# Prais
# Carlton M

"Easily the craziest, weirdest, strangest, funniest, most obscene writer in America."
—*GOTHIC MAGAZINE*

"Carlton Mellick III has the craziest book titles... and the kinkiest fans!"
—CHRISTOPHER MOORE, author of *The Stupidest Angel*

"If you haven't read Mellick you're not nearly perverse enough for the twenty first century."
—JACK KETCHUM, author of *The Girl Next Door*

"Carlton Mellick III is one of bizarro fiction's most talented practitioners, a virtuoso of the surreal, science fictional tale."
—CORY DOCTOROW, author of *Little Brother*

"Bizarre, twisted, and emotionally raw—Carlton Mellick's fiction is the literary equivalent of putting your brain in a blender."
—BRIAN KEENE, author of *The Rising*

"Carlton Mellick III exemplifies the intelligence and wit that lurks between its lurid covers. In a genre where crude titles are an art in themselves, Mellick is a true artist."
—*THE GUARDIAN*

"Just as Pop had Andy Warhol and Dada Tristan Tzara, the bizarro movement has its very own P. T. Barnum-type practitioner. He's the mutton-chopped author of such books as *Electric Jesus Corpse* and *The Menstruating Mall*, the illustrator, editor, and instructor of all things bizarro, and his name is Carlton Mellick III."
—*DETAILS MAGAZINE*

## Also by **Carlton Mellick III**

**Satan Burger**
**Electric Jesus Corpse**
**Sunset With a Beard** (stories)
**Razor Wire Pubic Hair**
**Teeth and Tongue Landscape**
**The Steel Breakfast Era**
**The Baby Jesus Butt Plug**
**Fishy-fleshed**
**The Menstruating Mall**
**Ocean of Lard** (with Kevin L. Donihe)
**Punk Land**
**Sex and Death in Television Town**
**Sea of the Patchwork Cats**
**The Haunted Vagina**
**Cancer-cute** (Avant Punk Army Exclusive)
**War Slut**
**Sausagey Santa**
**Ugly Heaven**
**Adolf in Wonderland**
**Ultra Fuckers**
**Cybernetrix**
**The Egg Man**
**Apeshit**
**The Faggiest Vampire**
**The Cannibals of Candyland**
**Warrior Wolf Women of the Wasteland**
**The Kobold Wizard's Dildo of Enlightenment +2**
**Zombies and Shit**
**Crab Town**
**The Morbidly Obese Ninja**
**Barbarian Beast Bitches of the Badlands**
**Fantastic Orgy** (stories)
**I Knocked Up Satan's Daughter**
**Armadillo Fists**
**The Handsome Squirm**

# THE CANNIBALS OF CANDYLAND

CARLTON MELLICK III

ERASERHEAD PRESS
PORTLAND, OREGON

ERASERHEAD PRESS
205 NE BRYANT
PORTLAND, OR 97211

WWW.ERASERHEADPRESS.COM

ISBN: 1-933929-85-5



Printed in the USA.

# AUTHOR'S NOTE

So I was wondering if I'm the only person who plays Candy Land and asks the questions: Are Princess Lolly and Lord Licorice doing each other? Does she sleep with Mr. Mint behind his back? What would their child look like if Mr. Mint impregnated Princess Lolly? Since they are made of candy, is it okay for the kids adventuring through candy land to eat the candy people? Do the candy people eat each other? Or do the candy people eat the kids? I'm not sure, but I sure as hell wouldn't go to Candy Land if it were a real place. You're bound to be eaten, or at least raped, by one of the natives.

One trend in literature that I really like is taking a classic children's fantasy and making it 'real' by placing it in our gritty perverted modern world. The book "The Emerald Burrito of Oz" by John Skipp and Mark Levinthal does this quite nicely. They basically ask the question: What if Oz was a real place that you could visit? Written for adults, the book gets into how our society has made an impact on the society of Oz. For example, the munchkins are all about sex, drugs, and punk rock.

Anyway, I decided I wanted to do the same thing with Candy Land. I kind of had the urge to write something similar to Razor Wire Pubic Hair, something dark and uncomfortably sexual, but set in Candy Land. As if the board game were based off of a real place, only in reality that place is dark and twisted. Not at all the happy world depicted in the game.

But, to tell you the truth, this book really isn't based on the board game at all. There is no Molasses Swamp or Gumdrop Pass, nor any character from Candy Land. It is set in a completely different world made of candy. If the board game was never invented I don't think this story would have been any different. Still, it's fun to draw lines between the two.

I spent New Year's Eve locked in a hotel, writing this book. Drunken teenagers dressed as anime characters were running around screaming in the streets below me as I wrote about red vine whips and marshmallow puppies. I had a box of jujubes with me for inspiration, and learned that jujubes are perhaps the worst candy of all time. The person who invented them needs to be punched in the face. Twice.

**- Carlton Mellick III, 06/23/09 4:32 pm**

# CHAPTER ONE

Franklin hates children, loves animals, and is deathly afraid of the candy people.

He also hates: riding the bus, talking to people on the phone, talking to people in person, dancing, getting haircuts, modern politics, the sound of vacuum cleaners, popular men's fashion, getting stared at, getting presents, having a boss, Chinese food, and his two wives.

He also loves: walking around downtown, playing with the puppies at pet stores, reading history books, listening to Mozart and death metal, watching the sound of autumn leaves rustling in the wind, making sandwiches, talking about books, blowing up balloons, historical politics, growing older, giving presents, working for himself, chess, Korean food, and wearing red.

He is also afraid of: pretty much everything.

Red is his favorite color. All of his clothes are red. He likes a particular shade of red that he calls apple-red. It is a bright red with a hint of orange.

His wives always say: "Your clothes are too orange-ish to be called apple-red."

He always responds: "When I was a boy, my parents had a tree in the front yard that grew apples of this color."

His wives always shake their heads at him.

Franklin walks down the sidewalk in his apple-red suit, wearing red gloves, a red baseball cap, and holding a red umbrella over his head. He shines loudly at every person who passes him. The people in his neighborhood have grown used to his glowing attire, but whenever he enters a new part of the city he can feel everyone's eyes on him. This is a bad part of Chinatown and not the kind of place where you'd want to stand out. A small gang of what Franklin believes to be Triads eye him from across the street near the entrance of an Asian strip club. If it wasn't raining they probably would confront him. Franklin has been beaten up twice just for wearing his red suit. Once by skinheads because they thought he was gay. Once by a couple of Chinese drug dealers because his clothes pissed them off, and because he walked on their sidewalk without the intention of buying any of their drugs.

He closes his umbrella and enters a pawn shop. Jake, the fat crooked-lipped owner of the shop, squints his puffy eyes at him as he approaches the counter. They nod at each other.

"In the back," Jake says.

Franklin wipes water out of his soul patch as he steps behind the counter into the back room. It is filled with cardboard boxes, broken appliances, a glass case full of swords, and an over-used sex doll with Judy Jetson hair.

"Adam wasn't fucking around when he said I'd recognize you," Jake says, flapping his arms to air out his yellow-stained armpits. "That suit is one of a fucking kind."

It wasn't exactly a compliment, but Franklin smiles as if it were. "I have all my clothes tailored in Argentina."

"Whatever floats your boat." Jake pulls a beer out of a mini-fridge and sits down in a rubber chair. He doesn't offer Franklin a seat. "Some people blow all their money on strippers. Some people blow it all on faggy outfits."

Franklin clears his throat. His hands hide in his pockets.

"Okay, let's see what I've got for you," Jake says. He opens up the casing of a broken VCR and pulls out a pistol wrapped in a white cloth. He unwraps it and presents the weapon to Franklin.

Franklin's left hand curls around the cold metal barrel and he picks it up like a hatchet. Then he places it into his right hand.

"How does it feel?" Jake says.

Franklin nods at the gun and rubs his fingers against it.

"That there is a Walther PPK," Jake says.

Franklin says, "Wasn't Adolf Hitler's gun a Walther PPK?"

"Where'd you read that?" Jake says.

"I'm kind of a history buff." Franklin smiles and hands the gun back.

"So you don't want it?"

"No, thank you," Franklin says. "I'm not interested in a Nazi gun."

"This is a common weapon," Jake says. "It wasn't just used by Nazis. James Bond also used a Walther PPK. Don't you like James Bond?"

"My grandmother was a holocaust survivor."

"So was my wife's family. What's the big deal?"

Franklin shakes his head.

"Didn't Adolf Hitler kill himself with his Walther PPK? Just think of it as the gun that killed Hitler."

"Don't you have anything that's not so antique. Something newer?"

"I only sell classics," Jake says. "Adam said you were a collector. I don't sell them for any other reason. No fucking way."

"I'm a collector."

"I'm just doing the community a service," Jake says. "Ever since the pussyfart liberal government took away our second amendment, us collectors had to move underground. I'm not in the business of selling arms to street thugs or to vengeful husbands who want to kill their cheating wives."

"You sell bullets, though, right?" Franklin says.

"Of course I do," Jake says.

"Okay, how much?" Franklin says.

"Look, I don't think I even want to sell it to you now. You look like a fucking wife-killer."

"How do I look like a wife-killer?"

"You look like the kind of guy who gets cheated on all the time."

"I'm not going to kill my wife," Franklin says. "It's for protection. Maybe I'm not a collector, but I need this."

Jake gives him a deep stare.

"Look me in the eyes," he says.

Franklin looks him in the eyes.

"I can tell if a fuck is being dishonest if I look him in the eyes." Jake blows snot into his fingers as he moves in closer. "Now tell me, what do you need the gun for?"

"Protection."

"Bullshit," Jake says. "Who do you want to kill with this? Your wife?"

"Not my wife."

Jake leans back and rubs the back of his neck, exposing crusty gray armpit hair. "Okay. Let's say I believe you. If not your wife, then who? The guy who's fucking her? Your boss? Some guy who owes you money?"

"No," Franklin says. "I would never kill a human being."

"But you're interested in killing," Jake says. "I see it in your eyes."

"I would never kill another human being."

"You're not..." Jake says. "You're not one of those candy man hunters are you?"

Franklin breaks eye contact with the fat man. Just for a split second, but the fat man notices.

"You are, aren't you?"

Franklin pets something furry in his pocket. "Yeah, so?"

"You believe in the candy people, too?"

"Yeah… do you?"

"I've seen some weird shit," Jake says. "But I've never seen any fucking candy people. There's a big part of me that thinks it's all a bunch of bullshit, but there's a little part of me that isn't quite sure." He cracks open another beer. "A lot of people come to me wanting to buy guns to protect their kids from the candy people. They tell me they've actually seen those things up close. I've looked them right in the eyes and not a single one of them has ever lied to me. Whether they exist or not, I have no fucking clue. But I've met a lot of people who truly believe they are real."

"They are definitely real," Franklin says, leaning in closer to Jake's eyes. "I promise you. They are real. And I am going to kill every last one of those bastards."

Jake stares at him for a few minutes and snorts. Then he pulls three boxes of bullets out of the VCR.

"In that case," Jake says. "Let me give you a little piece of advice. Shoot them at close range. You won't be able to break through their hard candy-coating unless you shoot them at close range or get a more powerful weapon."

Franklin nods and hands him an envelope. As Jake counts the money, Franklin examines the swords in the glass case and something catches his fancy. It is bright red, almost an apple-red.

He turns to the fat man and asks, "How much for the red cane sword?"

# CHAPTER TWO

Franklin was named after Franklin Pierce, the 14th President of the United States. Franklin Pierce is known as one of the worst presidents in the history of the country, for doing nothing to stop the rising tension between the North and the South in the days before the Civil War. He just wasn't a strong leader. He was the wrong person to be in charge of the country at that time in history.

When he was young, Franklin always wondered why his parents named him after the worst president in history, but they wouldn't tell him why. He studied the president, looked for a good side of him, looking for a reason as to why they would have named him after this particular man. Franklin Pierce was handsome, young, well-spoken, well-liked, and won the presidency in a landslide. He also accomplished quite a bit in the realm of foreign policy. Unfortunately, he just wasn't up to the task of being president.

After reading more about the president, Franklin started feeling sorry for the guy. Not only is he known as the worst president in history, he also lived a very tragic life. Two of his children died of diseases when they were very young. Then, two months before Pierce went into office, his third and final child was killed in a train accident. Jane Pierce, the president's wife, blamed her son's death on her husband's political ambitions. During her stay in the White House, she went into a state of mental anguish. She spent most of her time locked in a room, all by herself, writing letters to her dead son. While in office, his wife turned on him, his political party turned on him, and even his Vice-President died forty-five days into office and was never replaced. Eventually, Franklin Pierce turned to alcoholism. It is believed that he killed an old woman while driving a carriage drunk one night. It is also believed that he drank himself to death after his wife died of tuberculosis.

Franklin still wonders why his parents named him after this man. He wonders if they did so because Pierce was such a pathetic, tragic figure in history. He wonders if his parents viewed his birth as a tragic event in their lives. Perhaps they didn't want him, and he ruined all of their hopes and dreams. Or perhaps they just wanted to name him after a president and chose the most handsome one they could find, without bothering to do any research on the man.

With his umbrella tucked under his arm, his red cane (which contains a hidden sword) tapping with his footsteps, petting the inside of one of his pockets, he walks through the wet streets of Old Town to get back home. On the way, he runs into four children playing a game of can hockey in the street. Can hockey is somewhat similar to regular hockey, but instead of a puck they use a crushed beer can, instead of a stick they use their legs, and instead of a goalie box they draw lines in the road with chalk rock. They don't use skates or helmets. It is a game Franklin used to play with his siblings when he was a kid, before they were brutally murdered.

These kids are Franklin's neighbors. He sees them playing in the street all the time, at all hours of the day, even at three in the morning. He tries to ignore them as he passes, but they stop playing their game when they see him in his bright red suit and chase after him. Their legs seem to be too short for their bodies, even for children. Franklin has noticed this in the past. It seems that most children around their age tend to have this genetic flaw. Although the news channels have never mentioned it, Franklin believes it has something to with the fetus-enhancing drugs that doctors are persuading pregnant mothers to take these days.

"Let me see it," one of the short-legged boys shouts at Franklin. The one with the thick-rimmed glasses.

"Not today," Franklin says.

"Aww, come on," the little one says.

The little one is the nice one. His name is Jimmy. The brat with the thick-rimmed glasses is named Troy. He doesn't know what the other two are called.

"Just show it to us, bitch," Troy says.

Franklin keeps walking.

"Just for a second you pussy bitch," Troy says. "You want me to call the cops and tell them you tried to touch my dick?"

Troy always threatens to call the cops on Franklin with child molestation charges if he doesn't do what he wants. Because of this, Franklin often ends up buying the kid expensive toys or renting him R-rated horror movies. He doesn't know what else to do.

Jimmy tugs on Franklin's red coat.

"I just want to pet him once," he says. "Just for a second."

Franklin lets out a puff of air.

"Fine," Franklin says. "Just one second."

He opens up his coat and a small kitten pokes its head out of the inside pocket. Its fur is red, white, and green. Candy-colored.

Jimmy's eyes light up. As he pokes his finger towards the kitten's fur, the kitten deflects it with a lick of its scratchy tongue. This cat isn't actually a kitten. It is a midget cat. It is a fully-grown five-year-old cat that is stuck in the body of a chubby little kitten with plump cheeks, frizzy fur, and scratchy high-pitched meows.

"Her name is Crabcake."

Jimmy pets Crabcake on the head and she closes her eyes and smiles at him. A kitty smile.

"She's a cutie!" Jimmy says.

Troy pulls a BB Gun out of his orange Naruto backpack and pumps the handle.

"Hold it there, Jimmy," Troy says as he pumps the pistol. "I'm going to shoot it out of his hands."

Franklin hides Crabcake inside of his coat.

"Fucking psycho," Franklin says to the kid and jogs away from them.

The kid gets angry. "Wait! I didn't say you could leave!"

Franklin picks up his pace, holding Crabcake firmly inside his pocket.

"Fucking faggot!" Troy yells. "Run away, you faggot!"

Troy shoots his BB gun at Franklin's back. Even though the BB just bounces off of Franklin's suit, it still hurts him enough that he lets out a small yelp. Besides Jimmy, all of the kids laugh at him. They chase after him and take turns firing the gun at his back until he gets inside of his apartment building.

Troy is the reason why Franklin hates children.

# CHAPTER THREE

Franklin lives in a tiny studio apartment in Old Town with two women that hate him: his wife and his wife's mother. He calls them his wives because it feels like he has two wives whenever they're both around. His wife, Sarah, looks very old for her age. Her mother, Susan, looks very young for her age. They look almost like twins. He isn't sleeping with either of them. He tries to distance himself from them. The only thing they want from him is his money, which is never enough to satisfy them.

When he enters the flat, he finds Sarah and Susan having sex with another man. They regularly sleep with other men, but they're usually a bit more discrete than doing it froggy-style on the rug in the entryway. They also regularly share the same lover, but they usually don't fuck him at the same time.

Franklin assumes they were hoping that he would walk in on them, so he tries to act as if it doesn't faze him. He steps over their wriggling legs and crosses the room to his box. Besides the bathroom, his box is the only private area in the studio. It is a homemade cubicle he constructed for himself using sheets of plywood for the walls. He also uses a blanket for a ceiling and door, so that his wives can't see what he's up to. To block out the sound, he listens to death metal on his headphones (which he initially only listened to because it was the loudest music he could think of, but he has strangely grown to enjoy it). It is the closest thing he has to a private room. His wives don't ever bother him while he's in his box, as long as he promises to never bother them anywhere else in the apartment.

Franklin unfolds an aluminum chair and sits down at his small elementary school desk. He turns on a reading lamp attached to the side wall and pulls out his bottom-line laptop from the cubbyhole. After it powers up, he plugs his headphones in and listens to some Human Remains MP3s to block out the sound of sex in the room. He turns the volume up as loud as it goes, but he can still hear Sarah screaming at the tops of her lungs as if she is purposefully trying to be heard over the music.

His wireless card doesn't pick up any unsecured networks at the moment, so he's unable to log onto the internet. This annoys him because there have been a lot of candy people sightings in the past few days and he's been wanting to track them or see if there have been discussions about them on the message boards.

He lets out a puff of air and looks at the mess of notes and maps that are pinned to the wooden walls of the cubicle. His entire life has been dedicated to tracking down the candy people. Ever since he dropped out of college, it has been his primary obsession. He has other obsessions, such as reading historical biographies and inventing new types of sandwiches, but proving the existence of the candy people is the only thing that's really important to him.

Crabcake wakes up and climbs out of his coat. She yawns a crackling meow as she crawls into his lap and goes back to sleep. Franklin rubs her belly with his free hand.

Franklin has given up a lot in his pursuit of the candy

people. He dropped out of school to hunt the candy people. He's lost several jobs because he was too focused on the candy people. He's given up most of his free time to hunt the candy people.

He also married Sarah instead of his first love, Staci, just because Sarah also believed in the candy people. He didn't like Sarah all that much but he thought he would be happier with somebody who could relate to his obsession. He didn't know that she was a compulsive liar before they were married, and that all of the encounters with the candy people she told him about were complete fabrications. If it wasn't for his obsession he wouldn't have married Sarah, which was one of the biggest mistakes of his life.

He also moved to this neighborhood, even though it's very small and the rent is very high, just because this area has the highest concentration of candy man sightings in the country.

Franklin takes the gun out of his coat and hides it in some dirty underwear. He knows his wives won't go anywhere near his underwear. Then he removes his right ear and pushes a small yellow button on the side of his head. The back of his skull opens like a sunflower, revealing his swollen oily brain.

Besides giving up his personal life to the hunting of candy people, he has also given up his natural human brain and had it replaced with a more advanced artificial brain. He spent all of his inheritance on the operation. The brain is made of silicon-based imitation neural tissue that works as a hybrid between computer and brain. It has given him a picture-perfect memory, the math skills of a calculator, advanced deduction and puzzle-solving skills, superior eye/hand coordination, and the ability to think or read twenty times faster than anyone else can speak. He can also beat any video game without losing a single life, most of the time.

Although he assumed the brain would be a major benefit in the hunt for candy people, it hasn't yet been much use to him. His two wives approved of the operation because they thought he would be able to get a high-paying job with his new brain, but that didn't happen to be the case. Companies stopped hiring people with artificial brains a few years ago, after they discovered all the defects. Almost five thousand people received the operation before anyone realized that the brains don't last as long as normal human brains. They have a tendency of breaking down, freezing, or frying in the way that most computers do after a few years. Many people who have had the operation had their memories wiped, some had lost senses or had their senses swapped so that they saw what they smelled and felt what they tasted, some had become vegetables, and many have gone completely insane without warning. Nothing has happened to Franklin yet but the doctors told him that it is only a matter of time. He might have three days, three years, or three decades. Nobody knows for sure. But they do know that it will happen someday and there is nothing that can be done to stop it.

Much of the skin on Franklin's face is plastic. They had to remove his ears, the skin on his scalp and his forehead or else the flesh would rip every time he opened his head to let his brain breathe.

That is one of the things Franklin likes most about his artificial brain… letting it breathe. His brain overheats once or twice a day, sometimes three or four times during periods of high stress. When this happens, he has to open up his skull and let it air out for ten minutes or so. Airing out his brain is incredibly relaxing to Franklin. It is like having a strong brandy and a good cigar at the end of a long day.

As his brain pulses against the cool draft, Franklin closes

his eyes, strokes his purring candy-colored cat, and listens to the screeching music on his headphones that has become as calming as white noise.

# CHAPTER FOUR

Franklin Pierce is self-employed. He makes his living teaching pet owners how to give the Heimlich maneuver and CPR to their dogs. It has strangely been a profitable venture for him. People care a lot more for their pets than he thought. At first, he wanted to make money by selling a manual on pet care. He wrote a book called "How to Save Your Best Friend's Life: A Do it Yourself Guide to Pet Paramedics." The book teaches people how to save their pets from choking, drowning, heart attacks, bleeding to death, and other such emergencies that require quick action in order to save a pet's life. He sold a lot of copies in pet shops and local bookstores, but found that more people were interested in taking lessons in person rather than reading his manual. So he started teaching lessons. He gives a group class twice a month and teaches private lessons almost daily.

Today Franklin is giving a private lesson to an old lady with a large angry Doberman who lives in the West Hills. When he arrives at her house, he meets a frowning overweight purple-haired woman wearing a large red bow and a flowery dress.

"Take off those shoes and that smile," she says to him.

She tells him that her dog gets angry whenever he sees someone smile.

Franklin complies. As he takes off his shoes, he hears Crabcake meowing from outside. Although he takes his kitty with him everywhere he goes, he never takes her into a client's home. He's never sure how his client's pet will react to her, so he always keeps her by the mailbox.

"Here he is," the old woman says as she presents her dog.

Franklin lets out a puff of air as he sees the dog. The animal matches the old woman in every way. It is old, overweight, and wears a flowery bandana with a red bow. It even has purple hair.

The dog growls at Franklin. As he usually does whenever he gets nervous, Franklin puts his hands in his pockets. Normally he does this to pet Crabcake, whose soft purr relaxes him, but this time he doesn't have a kitty in his pocket. This time he has a gun. He pets the barrel of the gun and finds that it, too, relaxes him.

Franklin never wanted to buy a gun, even though he was hunting the Candy people. All he wanted to do was capture a candy person on film and then prove to the world that they exist. Once the world accepts that they do exist, he imagines the military will hunt them down and exterminate them all.

He has been successful at capturing them on tape three times. The first two times were not very clear. He got them from a distance, a safe distance, but they just looked like people in crazy-colored clothing. Even the community of candy man hunters online didn't believe they were real. Even he wasn't sure about one of them. But the third time, he captured one of them perfectly. He was less than twenty feet away, on a balcony above it, and was able to zoom right into the creature's face. It was like the creature was posing for him and stood there for a good five minutes. It was a perfect shot. The best footage anyone had ever captured.

Franklin thought he had won. But, still, nobody believed his footage was real. The cops laughed at him. News stations wouldn't respond to his letters or phone calls. Some of his online buddies believed the footage to be real, but most of them were skeptical. That's when he decided that the only way to prove the candy people are real is to kill one of them and use the corpse as indisputable evidence. That's when he decided to buy a gun.

As he teaches the old lady how to save her grumpy dog's life in the case of an emergency, Franklin caresses the gun in his pocket. He imagines what it will feel like to shoot one of the candy people, blow apart their candy-coating, and splatter their guts all over the sidewalk. He wonders if killing just one of them would be enough to avenge the death of his little brother and sisters. He wonders if the military will do anything about them, or if he'll have to kill them all himself.

The Doberman growls at Franklin as his lips turn into a large wicked smile.

After his job is done and Franklin picks Crabcake up from the old lady's lawn, he sees something in the corner of his eye. It is something moving down the street towards a small neighborhood park. Something with bright colors that glitter in the sunlight.

When Franklin looks up, he sees pink cotton candy hair

disappear behind a grassy hill. And in the air, he smells something sweet and fruity, like a wet artificially flavored strawberry lollipop. It's the same thing he smelled when he met the candy person as a child, over twenty years ago.

# CHAPTER FIVE

Franklin encountered the candy person when he was ten years old. He was with his older sister, Hillary, who was twelve, his little brother, Andrew, who was nine, and his little sister, Laura, who was seven.

He had just finished playing basketball with Andrew in the park. He didn't like basketball, but his brother loved it and loved playing against Franklin because he always won. Andrew only liked to play games that he was guaranteed to win.

After the match, Andrew kept saying, "You got pwned!" over and over again. Pwned was Andrew's favorite slang word and used it as much as possible.

"I pwned the hell out of you!" Andrew said.

"Yeah, yeah," Franklin said.

"Don't swear," Hillary said.

"I didn't swear!" Andrew said. "Pwned isn't a swear word."

"I meant hell," Hillary said.

"Oh," Andrew said.

The four of them often visited the park. Andrew went because he liked to play basketball and climb trees. Hillary went because she liked to climb trees and make sure nobody got into any trouble. Laura went because she liked to get into trouble and find toadstools. Franklin went because their parents didn't like it when he stayed indoors, drawing pictures and reading books all day.

Franklin would rather have stayed home than gone to the park, but he didn't completely loathe the experience. He liked spending time with Laura, who was his favorite sibling. Although she was only seven, she was fearless, clever, and charismatic. Nobody could stop her from doing whatever she wanted to do, not even Hillary. She was everything that Franklin was not. He envied her.

While Andrew and Hillary went off to climb a big tree in the middle of the park, Franklin went with Laura to find toadstools. She liked toadstools because they reminded her of fairies.

"How about this one?" Franklin asked, pointing at a toadstool growing under a bench.

"Nah," Laura said. "It's too mundane."

"Mundane?" Franklin asked.

"It's boring and ordinary. I only want the ones that are special."

Franklin pointed at another one.

"How about that one," he said. "That one looks like a turtle!"

"Nah," Laura said. "That one is ugly and deformed. Only ugly fairies would sit on a toadstool like that. I want to find a pretty one so that a pretty fairy will sit on it."

Laura planned to put the toadstools she collected into a flowerpot and place it on her windowsill in the hope that a fairy might come and sit on one of them. Then she would catch the fairy, put it into a cage, and keep it as a pet. Having a pet fairy was what Laura wanted more than anything. The rest of the family thought it was kind of weird, but Franklin thought it was cute.

Laura and Franklin were the two weird ones in the family. Whenever Laura did anything weird, their parents would laugh. Whenever Franklin did anything weird, their parents would get angry. Franklin concluded that it was only okay to be weird if everyone already really likes you.

When Franklin found a toadstool with pink spots and a light blue hue, he knew it was just what Laura was looking for.

"How about this one?" he told her. "This one is perfect."

But Laura didn't look at it. Her eyes were focused on something else. Something much more interesting.

"What?" Franklin said when she would not respond.

He smelled the sweetness of strawberry lollipops in the air. Then he saw what Laura was looking at. A brightly colored woman, kind of like a clown, was walking through the grass towards them.

It was a woman made of sweet treats. She wasn't wearing any clothes, but her skin was coated in a layer of candy. She had pink cotton candy for hair, white taffy skin with cinnamon cheeks, plump gummy lips, a maraschino cherry nose, red and white striped legs like candy canes, shoulders made of chocolate, blue hands that looked like gloves of bubblegum ice cream, long butterscotch candy fingernails, a rainbow-swirled belly like a giant circus lollipop, and soft marshmallow breasts with gumdrops for nipples. She carried a jump rope of red licorice and a large white bag. The only things not made of candy were her eyes, but they were as pink as strawberry soda.

"Wow, she's pretty!" Laura cried. "I bet she has treats in her bag!"

Then Laura ran towards the candy lady.

Franklin knew something was wrong with the woman. He could sense it in the way she glared at him with her pink snake-like eyes and the way she curled her hard candy fingernails as if they were raven claws. Even though he sensed danger, he couldn't help but become drawn to the woman. The sweet smell in the air that filled his lungs was intoxicating. It warmed his mind with a calming bliss that took away all of his fears and worries. It pulled him towards the woman's heavenly sweetness.

Franklin saw that Andrew and Hillary were also drawn to the woman. They had climbed down from the tree and walked like drunken zombies towards her. They were even closer to her than Laura and looked to be twice as dazed.

It was Andrew who got to the woman first. He said hello to her and asked her for candy. She didn't speak. She took him by the shoulder and pulled him closer, allowing him to lick her sweet candy stomach. As he closed his eyes to lick, the woman wrapped her claws around him. That's when Franklin noticed her teeth. Although her outside was sweet and pleasant, her insides were nasty and horrific. Her tongue was like that of a snake's and her teeth were razor-edged nails.

The woman bit into Andrew's neck and tore out his throat. That's when Franklin snapped out of it. He screamed as he saw the woman tear into his little brother and thrash her head around like a shark ripping a chunk out of a seal. She made squealing growling noises as she thrashed at him. Franklin then realized she was more like a vicious animal than a human being.

Andrew's blood splashed into Hillary's face. She cringed and wiped the blood out of her eyes. It wasn't until she took her hands away from her face that she realized where she was and what was happening. She shrieked and turned around to run away, but she didn't get far. The candy woman whipped her red licorice vine at her and it wrapped around her throat.

The woman jerked it back like a fishing rod and Hillary's neck made a loud cracking sound. Then she fell limp to the ground.

Franklin turned to run, but Laura didn't follow him. She was still in a trance. Even though she just witnessed her brother and sister murdered by the woman, she was still drawn towards the candy smell. Franklin tried to pull her by the arm, but she resisted with all her strength. He tried to pick her up, but she kicked him as hard as she could in the stomach. He tried slapping her face, but she didn't seem to notice.

The woman dropped Andrew's body and stepped towards them. Blood dripped down her white candy chin as she exposed her teeth. Franklin pulled on Laura as hard as he could, but she would not move. Once the woman was within arms reach, he had no choice but to let his sister go and run for his life. He ran several yards away and then turned around. He watched as his sister embraced the candy woman like her own mommy, with a big smile on her face. His sister didn't even let out a whimper as the woman bit into her belly. It was like Laura was so drugged that she couldn't feel a thing. The candy woman kneeled over her, coated in gore, pulling her insides out and stuffing them in her mouth. Before she died, Laura turned her head and looked at Franklin. The big smile was still on her face like it was the happiest day of her life.

That's the image that burned in Franklin's memory. It is what he has seen every day when he goes to sleep at night, and every morning when he wakes up. He sees his little sister smiling at him as the creature made of candy squats over her open body, eating her innards.

The woman didn't come after Franklin. After she was done eating and after Laura had stopped moving, she gathered the remains of her victims into her large white bag. Then tossed it over her shoulder and walked away.

His parents never forgave him for surviving the encounter, nor did he ever forgive himself. He tried telling everyone about the candy woman, but they all thought he was delusional after such a tragic experience.

Outside of the old lady's house, Franklin pets the gun in his pocket and stares at the park at the end of the street. By the sweet scent in the air, he is pretty sure that it was a candy person who just went over that hill in the park. All he has to do is go after it, pull out his gun and shoot the creature dead. It's that easy. Then his sweet little Laura will be avenged.

But as much as he wants to, and needs to, he can't get himself to go after it. He shakes with excitement at the thought of revenge, but he doesn't go after it. He hesitates, makes excuses, tells himself that he just imagined the candy person. Then he lets out a puff of air. He takes his hand away from the gun in his pocket and uses it to pet his kitty and hug her tightly to his chest.

# CHAPTER SIX

Franklin spends the rest of the day hating himself for not having the courage to go after the candy person in the park. At one of the breweries downtown, he drinks a few Belgian-style ales. He only goes to the brewery once a month, because he can't afford it and because he doesn't get very buzzed anymore due to his artificial brain.

Drinking a Tripel, he pets Crabcake in his red suit pocket and wonders how many children will die because he let that thing live. He doesn't know why he hesitated. It was perfect timing, too. He had the gun with him and the neighborhood was mostly empty due to it being in the middle of a workday. He only runs into candy people a couple times a year at most. It might be three years before he sees one again. Then again, this was the second one he had run into in just a month. He wonders if they are hunting more frequently. Perhaps they are getting hungrier or perhaps they are growing in number.

After he finishes his beer, he asks the bartender with the Santa Claus tattoo for another abbey-style on cask.

"Sorry, buddy," the bartender says, shaking his head. "All out."

"Of the abbey?" Franklin says. "No you're not."

"The keg is cashed," says the bartender.

"You still have approximately one hundred and twenty-two ounces left in the cask."

The bartender shakes the cask. Beer splashes inside, but he still shakes his head. "Nope, empty."

"Look," Franklin says, taking off his apple-red hat and placing it onto the counter. "I can tell how many ounces are left in it based on the sound it makes when it is pumped. I know that you know there is more beer in the cask and you just don't want to give me anymore for some reason or another. If I had to guess I would say that this is the last of the batch. It is a really good beer. You probably want to take the rest of it home for yourself."

"It's not that," the bartender says. "You've just had too many beers already."

"But I've only had three beers," Franklin says.

"But each of those were over eight percent alcohol."

"But three glasses of wine isn't too much in restaurant and red wine is usually thirteen or fourteen percent."

The bartender squints his eyes and frowns at him.

"Look," Franklin says. "I just want one more beer. That leaves you one hundred and eight ounces left to take home. That is still plenty of beer."

"Yeah, but—" the bartender begins.

"You might have noticed I said one hundred and eight ounces rather than one hundred and six. If you poured me a normal sixteen-ounce pint there would only be one hundred and six ounces left, but you haven't been filling up any beers all the way to the top of any glasses you have been pouring which has been shorting people out of two ounces of beer per glass. I am okay with this. I don't like to complain. But if you will not give me another pint from the cask, I would at least like six ounces of it to make up for the beer I already paid for."

The bartender shakes his head at Franklin as if he were the biggest asshole customer he's had all week.

"Fine," the bartender says, and pumps him a beer from the cask.

When he gets the beer, he discovers it's six ounces short of a pint. The bartender still charges him for a full pint and quickly walks away to serve another customer before Franklin has the chance to complain about it.

On his way home, Franklin runs into Troy in the street again. This time the kid is all alone.

"Hey Fagboy," Troy says to Franklin. "Where the hell were you? I've been waiting for you all day."

Franklin ignores him and keeps walking.

"I need some money," Troy says. "Right now."

"I'm sorry, I'm broke," Franklin says.

"Right now!"

"I told you I don't have any money."

"You better have some money. Or else you know what's going to happen."

Franklin wonders if the kid knows he is lying.

"Look kid," he says. "I spent it all at the bar."

"You have to have some money. Just give me whatever you've got."

Franklin stops and turns to the kid. "What do you need it for, anyway?"

"It's Jimmy's birthday tomorrow. I want to get him that

new transformer he's been asking for. Our parents aren't going to give him shit."

"He's your little brother?" Franklin asks.

"Yeah," Troy says. "I look out for him."

Franklin stares at him for a moment. Then he nods his head.

"Okay," Franklin says. "I'll give you what I've got. But it's not much."

"Give me all of it," the kid says.

Franklin gives him seven dollars and some change.

Troy takes the money and runs off. Then he turns around and says, "Thanks, Fagboy!"

And when the kid turns around Franklin hears him say, "What a stupid bitch."

Franklin stands in the street for a few minutes, wondering if he has just been duped. Even with his fancy hi-tech brain, Franklin can't outsmart an eleven-year-old.

At home, Sarah and Susan are waiting for him. There is another guy with them, sitting on the couch. He might be the guy from the night before or maybe he's somebody else. The apartment is destroyed. It smells like smoke and pee. Franklin guesses they're on another meth binge. They always destroy the apartment when they go on a meth binge.

"What happened?" Franklin asks.

He notices that his handmade cubicle has been razed to the floor. Part of it is blackened as if they lit it on fire and then pissed the fire out, which would account for the smell of the room.

"We've made a decision," Susan says. "We want you to move out."

"Yeah," Sarah says.

"What did you do to my office?" Franklin says as he digs through the pee-soaked boards in the corner of the room.

"We burned it," Sarah says, giggling. "We burned all your stuff."

"You burned my clothes? My laptop?"

"We don't want you here anymore," Susan says. "You're a loser."

"I'm a loser?" Franklin says. "Neither of you have worked a day in your lives."

"Just get out," Susan says.

"This is my apartment," Franklin says. "My name is on the lease."

"We don't care," Susan says. "David just got kicked out of his place so he is moving in. The three of us decided that you should go."

"Who the hell is going to pay your rent then?" Franklin says. "If you think I am going to then you're even stupider than I realized."

"David will," Sarah says. "He has loads of money."

Franklin looks at the guy on the couch. He's much younger than any of them with long greasy black hair, a scraggly beard, and several homemade tattoos. He looks like a cross between a hippie and a Mexican gang member.

"What does he do?" Franklin says. "Sell drugs?"

"He makes more than you," Sarah says.

"Then why doesn't he get you guys a nicer apartment? I moved here for a reason. I'm staying. If you want to move in with your boyfriend, find another love nest."

"If you don't leave now we'll have David throw you out," Susan says.

"If you don't leave now I'll call the cops on your drug dealer boyfriend," Franklin says.

"What did you just say?" says a deep voice from the couch.

David stands up and faces Franklin. "Did you say you were going to call the cops on me?" He picks up Franklin's red cane from the floor. It is the only item of Franklin's that survived his wives' meth-crazed wave of destruction. Franklin hopes that the guy doesn't realize there is a sword inside.

Franklin pets the pistol in his pocket. "I'm not leaving."

"Yes, you are," David says.

Sarah cheers with glee as David swings the red cane like a baseball bat at Franklin's head. But with his quick eye-hand coordination, Franklin is able to duck out of the way and land a punch in the center of David's face. Although the punch hurt Franklin's hand far more than it hurt David, it pisses the hell out of the young drug dealer.

"You son of a bitch!" Sarah screams at Franklin.

"What the hell did you do that for?" Susan says.

Franklin doesn't understand why they are angry with him for defending himself.

David swings the cane another time and Franklin dodges it again. Franklin doesn't try to throw another punch, because his hand is suffering enough from the last one. Then his two wives join the fight. They throw their fists at his red suit and kick at his shins.

Franklin puts one hand in his pocket to protect Crabcake and with his free hand he reaches for the gun in his other pocket. But before he can pull out the gun, Susan punches him in the side of the head, right on his temple. His right ear pops off. He doesn't realize she has accidentally hit the button beneath his ear until he feels his skull opening up.

As Franklin takes his hand out of his pocket to retrieve

his artificial ear, he sees David's shadow behind him swinging the cane with all his strength. The cane slams into his exposed brain and Franklin blacks out.

# CHAPTER SEVEN

Franklin awakes in an alley a couple blocks away from his apartment. His mind is foggy. He feels the side of his head and discovers that his skull is still open. He gently touches his brain with the tips of his fingers. There are cigarette butts and bits of dirt stuck to his neural tissue. There is also a fluid coating it that shouldn't be there. He rubs some of the fluid with his fingers and smells it. It is human urine.

"What the..." Franklin yells. "Did they pee on my brain?"

He cringes as he tries to wipe the dirt and urine from the surface of his brain tissue, but every time he wipes it causes his mind to go fuzzy and warped. He cleans it the best he can and then pushes the button to close his skull. But his skull does not close.

Feeling the lids of his skull, he realizes that they've been jammed. Two pieces of the metal frame are bent. One of the pieces is dangling from its hinges. He'll need to get another operation to fix it. In the meantime, his brain will have to remain exposed.

He still has his gun, which is jabbing into the side of his stomach. His cane is on the ground next to him. His entire body is filled with sore spots, so his wives must have beat him with the cane while he lay unconscious in the alley. He no longer has his hat or his right ear. His umbrella is missing. And his cat, Crabcake, is not in his pocket.

He scans the alley for his kitten, but she is nowhere to be seen. This worries Franklin. Crabcake stays with him twenty-four hours a day. She never leaves his side even for a minute. Even if he had been laying in that alley for days, she would not have voluntarily left his side.

"They took her," Franklin says.

He gets to his feet. He knows the only way Crabcake wouldn't be with him is if his wives kept the cat or did something to it.

Franklin leaves the alleyway, holding the gun in his pocket, ready to draw the sword out of the cane. He doesn't care that his wives kicked him out of his apartment. He doesn't care that they burned his stuff. He doesn't care that they beat him and broke his skull lids. He doesn't even care that they peed on his brain. But if they did anything to his cat, he will kill them all without hesitation.

He thinks that Jake, the guy who sold him the gun, might have been right. Maybe he was going to kill his wife with the gun. It wasn't his original plan, but at this moment he is ready to kill someone.

As Franklin gets to the front of his apartment building, he hears a scream. A child's scream. He stops and looks around. The street is empty. Another scream. This one is a loud cry for help. Franklin steps away from the entrance of his apartment and follows the screams.

In a parking garage around the corner, he sees a little boy being eaten alive by a man made out of candy. The man has bulging swirly lollipop eyes and long black licorice hair that resemble dreadlocks. He wears a brown chocolate suit with jellybeans for buttons. The creature has ripped open the kid's chest and is gnawing on his ribcage. The boy cries for help as the man eats him alive. He would have seen Franklin over the creature's shoulder if his eyes hadn't been slurped out of his head.

Still dazed from the damage to his artificial brain, Franklin isn't thinking straight enough to be afraid. He pulls the gun from his pocket and points it at the candy man. Remembering what the gun dealer said about their candy skin, Franklin stumbles towards the candy man, aims for the head, and shoots him three times. Even though he's only twelve feet away, the bullets don't hit the creature in the head. One of them goes over its head. One of them grazes its soft caramel shoulder. But the third hits it in the side, cracking open its brown rootbeer-flavored candy coating.

The creature shrieks and leaps away from the boy. It sees Franklin. Its lollipop eyeballs swirl at him. Before Franklin can fire again, the creature turns and runs away. It moves as fast as a cat, leaping over the railing of the parking garage and down the street.

Franklin decides it isst better to help the boy than chase after the creature. The kid is in pieces. He is crying, coughing up blood. His ribs are exposed. Franklin can see his heart beating rapidly through the ribs.

"Don't worry," Franklin says. He kneels down and holds the kid's hand. "I'll get you help."

The boy stops crying and stares at Franklin with empty eye sockets.

"What time is it?" the boy asks.

Franklin isn't sure why the boy wants to know the time, but he looks at his watch and tells him anyway. "It's a little past midnight."

The kid smiles.

"That means it's my birthday now," he says.

Franklin then recognizes the kid. It is Jimmy. The little kid who wanted to pet Crabcake the previous day. The nice kid.

"That's why I went to the rootbeer man," he says. "I thought he was going to give me a present for my birthday."

The kid no longer seems to be in any pain. Franklin hopes he's just in shock.

"Troy promised me that somebody would get me a present this year," he says. "He wouldn't tell me who. I was hoping it would be a wizard or a lion tamer or someone magical like that. That's why I thought the rootbeer man might be the one. I didn't know he was going to be mean."

Franklin realizes that Jimmy isn't just in shock. The boy isn't feeling pain anymore because he is about to die.

"Jimmy," Franklin says. "The person who bought you a present was your brother, Troy. He told me today that he was going to buy you a transformer. The one you wanted."

The red holes in his head light up with excitement, as if they still had eyes in them.

"Really?" Jimmy cries.

"Yes," Franklin says. "But don't tell him that I told. He'll get mad at me for ruining the surprise."

"I can't wait," Jimmy says.

He sighs a deep happy sigh, but never draws another breath.

Franklin looks away from the boy's body and sees a trail of blood heading in the direction the candy man had fled.

As Franklin leaves the parking garage, his hands covered in Jimmy's blood, he runs into Troy. The boy sees the blood on Franklin's hands. Then he sees his little brother's ragged corpse in the deserted parking lot behind them. He puts two and two together and screams.

Franklin tries to calm him down, but the boy only screams louder. He screams for his mom and dad, as if they are just around the corner. Franklin tries to put his hand over the boy's mouth but the boy runs away, screaming for the police.

# CHAPTER EIGHT

Franklin runs down the street, following the trail of blood the wounded candy man left behind. He has to kill or capture this creature or else he'll never be able to prove his innocence to the police.

The trail leads him to a manhole near the old park. The park had been shut down a few years ago, because more children had gone missing at that park than any other park in the country. The manhole cover has not been closed properly, making it easier for Franklin to catch up to the creature. Franklin assumes the candy man must have been too injured to close it, but knows that it might also be a trap. The candy man might be down there, waiting for him in the dark.

Although he doesn't have a flashlight, Franklin decides to risk it and go down the ladder. He doesn't have much of a choice. The sewer is surprisingly large and dry. With the little light he has shining through the gutters, he's able to navigate through the tunnel. Following the trail of blood becomes difficult in the dim lighting, and then it becomes even more difficult once the sewer branches off into a maze of tunnels. He has to use all of his fancy brain to focus on the blood trail.

After a few blocks, he comes to another manhole. The lid is still open, just as the last one. Franklin climbs down to discover another maze of tunnels identical to the tunnels above. It is some kind of sub-sewer. Franklin isn't quite sure why there is another sewer below the regular sewer. He doesn't know very much about sewers. This sewer is much colder and darker than the previous one. He uses his cane to guide him forward in the dark. He cannot see any blood in this tunnel, so he moves towards a dim light in the distance. He figures that would be the most logical place the creature would be headed.

The light becomes brighter once he turns a corner, then even brighter once he turns another corner. Eventually he discovers where the light is coming from: another manhole.

He climbs down the ladder. This one goes deeper down than the previous two. The maze of tunnels here are surprisingly clean and very bright. They are lit with some kind of iridescent lighting in the corners of the walls. Franklin can see the trail of blood perfectly now. He walks with his gun pointing forward. The tunnel branches every thirty feet. The blood trail twists through the tunnels in a disorderly fashion. It ends in the middle of a white wall. A bloody handprint centers the wall.

Franklin puts his left hand over the handprint and pushes. The wall opens up like a revolving door. Beyond the door is a tiny room with a red spiral staircase heading downwards. Once he sets his foot onto the first step of the staircase he recognizes that it is made of hard candy.

He takes the ladder down, careful not to slip on any of the blood. Franklin calculates that the stairs go down for eighty-eight feet. At the bottom, Franklin finds himself surrounded by rock walls. The blood leads into the mouth of a brightly lit cave. Franklin moves faster. He needs to catch up to the wounded candy man before he reaches any of his friends.

The farther Franklin goes, the wider the cave gets and deeper into the earth it descends. He keeps his eyes on the blood and his gun pointed forward. Soon the cave opens up into another world. Franklin has to stand still to take it all in. As far as his eyes can see, there is a landscape of bright colors and swirling patterns. A landscape made out of candy.

There are lollipop trees, licorice grass, cotton candy clouds in a grape-flavored purple sky, hills made of chocolate, rivers of jelly, fields of candy canes, and in the far distance there are enormous blue, green, and pink gumballs the size of mountains.

Franklin picks up his pace. He climbs over hills of chocolate, careful not to slip in the peanut butter mud, and enters a meadow by a pond filled with watermelon soda. On the other side of a pond, Franklin sees the wounded candy man crawling through the marshmallow flowers. He has lost too much blood and can no longer move very quickly. The candy man looks back at Franklin with cold lollipop eyes, breathing hoarsely and drooling blood.

Not wasting any time, Franklin crosses the meadow until he is standing above the creature, pointing his gun down on it. The creature stares at Franklin with its mouth wide open, his rough breaths sound like growls.

"You are an ugly thing," Franklin tells the candy man. "It's time you were put out of your misery."

He aims for the creature's heart.

"No, you are an ugly thing," says the candy man. His voice is like that of an old sailor's.

Franklin steps back. He wasn't expecting the thing to understand English. He always assumed that these creatures were more like animals than people.

"You can speak?" Franklin asks.

"Of course I can speak," says the candy man. "I am a man, am I not?"

"Not exactly," Franklin says.

"We are not that much different from you," he says.

The creature holds in his wound as he speaks. His cracked candy coating crumbles between his fingers.

"What are you people?" Franklin asks.

"What do you think we are?" says the man. "We are candy people."

"Where do you come from?"

"We come from the same place as you," says the candy man. "My people were once human like you, but we evolved differently. We evolved into candy people."

"How can somebody evolve into candy?" Franklin asks, lowering his gun. "It doesn't make any sense."

"Just as spiders evolved to produce webs to catch flies, just as cheetahs evolved to run faster to catch antelope, just as lantern fish evolved to produce lights that attract smaller fish to their mouths, we evolved into candy people so that it would be easier for us to catch our prey: children. Our ancestors were a community of cannibals, who used to lure children with candy. After several generations, our young ones were born with candy growing from their hands. Eventually they were born with candy skin. It is the way of evolution."

Franklin doesn't know if he can believe him. He wonders if he is just a normal man wearing a costume made of candy. He wonders if they are just a community of insane cannibals, who created an underground environment to look like it was made of candy. It would make much more sense to him than evolution.

"That kind of evolution takes a very long time," Franklin

says. "Millions of years."

"Not in our case, it seems," the man says.

Franklin lets out a puff of air.

"But how do you know English?" Franklin says. "How do you know about lantern fish and cheetahs?"

The candy man coughs a laugh. "As I said, our people were once humans. They spoke English. They had books. We learned from these books. We are an educated people."

"You are monsters," Franklin says.

"We are no more monsters than you are," says the man.

"You eat children," Franklin says.

The candy man shrugs.

"Well, yes," he says. "They are delicious."

Franklin spits at him. "You evil piece of—"

As Franklin raises his gun to the creature's head, the candy man lunges at him. The gun goes off, but the bullet misses. The candy man stabs him with his rootbeer-flavored fingernails. Although made of candy, the fingernails are as strong as glass and as sharp as knives. Franklin cries out. He points his gun at the candy man's stomach and fires twice, throwing the creature back.

The candy man shrieks. He raises his claws and goes for Franklin's throat, but Franklin gets him first. He fires three bullets into the creature's head at point blank range. A fleshy human brain explodes out of the candy skull in blubbery chunks. The creature falls back. The blue swirl in his lollipop eyes goes white.

# CHAPTER NINE

Franklin falls into the marshmallow flowers, holding his stomach. He looks around to see if any other candy people are in the area. The gunshots would surely attract attention. He's out of bullets. The rest of the bullets are hidden in his apartment. He doesn't know what he's going to do if other candy people show up. His cane sword is his only defense.

He decides to act quickly. Even though his insides feel like they've been shredded into pulp, he drags the corpse of the candy man across the meadow. He is much heavier than a normal human. Franklin can tell the candy coating adds another 53.7 pounds.

He winces as he drags the body and cries out whenever he slips in a puddle of caramel or vanilla frosting. Then he hears pounding footsteps coming towards him from the other side of the hill. He pulls harder, but it only makes him lose his balance against the terrain and fall down more frequently. The gun slips out of his pocket, but he decides to leave it. He doesn't need it anymore. All he needs is to get out of there alive and bring this body to the police.

The noises that are coming closer no longer sound like footsteps to Franklin. They are more like thumping sounds, like somebody is dribbling a dozen basketballs at once.

Franklin sees a group of multi-colored blobs the size of beach balls bouncing over the hill towards him. They are cherry, orange, lemon, lime, and grape balls of living gummy candy. Though they have no limbs, the candies each have a single eye in the center of their bodies and large mouths.

Franklin doesn't know what to make of them. He is more surprised than afraid. Just to be on the safe side, Franklin moves quickly away from the gummy blobs, pulling the body with all his strength. But the creatures follow him. They catch up and swarm him, bouncing up and down around, circling him like little gummy sharks.

The blobs block his path and force him to stop. He smacks at one of them with his cane, but it just comes right back. He smacks another one, but it catches the cane in its mouth and won't let go. Franklin swings the little blob through the air, but it is stuck to the cane like a leech, making slurping noises.

An orange blob wraps its mouth around the candy man's foot and bites it off. The creature doesn't actually have any teeth, but it is still somehow able to suck the foot off of the candy man's leg with ease. The gummy creature is transparent, so Franklin can see the candy man's foot inside of the blob as it bounces around.

The rest of the blobs attack. They bounce in and take bites out of the dead candy man's flesh and bounce out. They do not attack Franklin, so he assumes they are only after the corpse. Half of the body is absorbed into the bellies of the blobs within minutes. Franklin knows this isn't good. If he doesn't get the body back home nobody will believe his story.

He jerks his cane with all his strength, sending the blob attached to the handle across the meadow. Then he smacks at any creature that comes close to the body. He knocks some of them back, but there are just too many of them. For every one he knocks away, three more come in from behind and take bites out of the corpse. Franklin pulls the sword out of the cane and stabs one of them with it, but the blob doesn't die. The hole seals itself up right away and the creature suffers no damage, not even pain.

Franklin knows that he can't give up, so he continues fighting them. He tries cutting the blobs in half, or stabbing them in their eyes, but they just reform themselves and continue their attack. Then the blobs stop going after just the corpse, and start going after Franklin. When he notices this, Franklin drops the body and backs away. Half of the blobs stay with the body, the other half come after him.

Within moments, the gummy blobs gobble up the rest of the corpse and Franklin finds himself surrounded again by the bouncing creatures. He chaotically thrashes his cane at the swarm and hits a lemon blob so hard that it knocks the cane out of his hand. Then the blobs charge in at him. He leaps over a cherry blob and runs for a giant candy cane growing out of the earth. Before they can take a piece out of him, he climbs up the candy pole to safety.

The blobs stay at the foot of the candy cane for an hour, bouncing hungrily up and down at him. Franklin sweats. At first, the moisture causes the candy cane to become sticky, which makes it easier for him to hold. But he sweats more and the candy cane becomes slick. He slides down the candy pole, and quickly climbs back up, only to slide down again. It takes only a few minutes before he loses his grip and falls into the swarm of gummy predators.

As he hits the ground, a blob jumps onto Franklin's chest. It is a fat purple blob that drools grape-flavored saliva as it opens its wide smiling mouth around Franklin's head. There is a cracking sound and the grape blob is thrown off of Franklin's chest and flies twenty-one feet into the air.

Lifting himself up, Franklin sees that someone has come to his rescue. A woman with a long red licorice whip flips through the air and lands on a chocolate malt ball nearby. She whips at the gummy blobs, sending them flying in all directions. The blobs scatter. The sound of the cracking whip seems to frighten them. They aren't sensitive to pain, they are sensitive to noise. His rescuer just has to crack the whip a few more times and the rest of the gummy blobs flee into the lollipop forest.

Franklin looks at the woman. It is a candy woman. She walks towards him with red and white striped legs, her red vine whip thrown over her shoulder, and a big smile on her face. When she rubs her fingers through her cotton candy hair, Franklin recognizes her. She is the woman from his childhood. The one that murdered his brother and sisters. The one that ruined his life.

He goes for his cane sword on the ground, but when he comes

up she is already standing in front of him, smiling at him.

"Are you cinnamon?" the candy woman says to Franklin. Her voice sounds like that of a cartoon elf. "I love cinnamon."

She smells him and rubs her hand along his red suit. "Or are you candy apple?"

Franklin backs away from her. She smiles at his shyness and he becomes paralyzed at the sight of her razor-sharp teeth. She steps closer to him. The smell of artificial strawberry fills his nostrils. It intoxicates him even more than it did when he was a child. His eyes drift into a state of bliss. She smells him again and her face becomes confused.

"I don't smell candy apple or cinnamon or anything," she says. "What's your name?"

He wants to cut her in half with his cane sword while she is off guard, but finds himself responding to her question.

"Franklin," he says, stepping closer towards her.

"What kind of candy is that?" she asks.

"It's not a candy, it's my name," he says.

"You mean you weren't named after a type of candy?" she says. "I thought everyone was named after candy."

"No," Franklin says.

"Huh…" she says, leaning her hand on her glossy hip. "Well, my name is Jujube, but you can call me Jujy."

The candy woman steps around Franklin and examines him.

"Hey, your brain is showing," she says to him when she walks behind him.

"I know," Franklin says.

She pokes at his brain a little, but stops once Franklin shakes her fingers away.

"Sorry," she says.

As Franklin sways in the drunken delight, Jujy licks him on the shoulder.

"Your candy-coating doesn't have any flavor at all!" she cries.

"I'm sorry," he says.

"Wait a minute..." she says.

Jujy leans her white taffy face into Franklin's. He looks into her pink eyes.

"You're not made of candy, are you?" she says. "You're one of those grownup children!"

Franklin steps away from her as her eyes grow wide. She steps towards him as he steps back, so that the distance between them remains the same.

"I've never tasted one of you before," she says, licking her red gummy lips at him.

In his intoxicated state, Franklin doesn't push her away as she wraps her arms around him and bites into the side of his neck. While his blood leaks down her sugar-white neck, he breathes in so much of her strawberry fragrance that his mind rolls into a soft, comfortable, dream.

# CHAPTER TEN

When Franklin awakes, he finds himself hanging from a cookie ceiling, his wrists tied together with black licorice as strong as leather. His mind is still cloudy. His vision smeared. Focusing his eyes on something moving on the floor. It is white and fluffy. When his eyes clear, he recognizes it as some kind of animal. It is a puppy made of marshmallow. The puppy is attacking a large bright red jawbreaker like it's a tennis ball.

Franklin examines the rest of the room. The walls all seem to be made of chocolate chip cookie dough that was baked into bricks. The carpet is furry brown sugar. The windows, made of thin hard candy, look like multi-colored stained glass. In the corner of the room, there is a bright yellow bed with pink flower patterns. Franklin isn't sure what it is made of but it looks more rubbery than it does soft. His red cane is on the far end of the room, leaning against the wall. He wishes it was within arm's reach.

Through the doorway in front of him, he sees the candy woman sitting at a table made of chocolate-covered wafers. She is holding a human leg in her hands and ripping chunks of meat off with her teeth. As she chews the raw flesh, she looks up and notices Franklin awake. She stares at him with her cold strawberry soda eyes, blood dribbling down her white chin.

With her mouth full, she says, "Your meat is not as tender as a child's."

Then she swallows and takes another bite.

Franklin looks down and discovers that his right leg is missing. There is a peppermint wood saw on the floor covered in blood. In his sleep, she had sawed off his leg and cauterized it with hot caramel sauce. Examining himself closer, he finds other chunks of meat hae been taken out of him. They are just small bites, like the one on his neck. All of his wounds are filled with hot caramel sauce. The strawberry fragrance fills the room, numbing his senses to the pain.

"What have you done…" Franklin says.

She swallows her food and wipes blood from her gummy lips.

"I've saved you," she says.

Franklin looks at his cane nearby. If only he could reach it he would have a weapon.

"My leg…" Franklin cries.

She lifts his leg to him, as if she thought he was asking to see it. Half of the meat is gone. Franklin can see the exposed muscles and tendons. The limb doesn't look familiar to him anymore. It looks like a piece of roadkill that the woman is eating raw. The only thing that Franklin recognizes is the apple-red pant leg covering the bottom of the limb like a burrito wrapper.

"It's a little too chewy," she says, picking at a piece of meat between her teeth. "And I don't like all the hair."

"Then why…" Franklin can't complete a full sentence.

"Oh, I'm sorry!" she says, acting very defensive all of a sudden. "It tastes really good! I don't think it's gross or anything. I was just comparing the differences between your meat and children meat. Your meat is still good… just different."

Her taffy cheeks blush into cinnamon redness. Then she awkwardly takes a large bite of his leg and acts as if it is the most delicious thing she has ever tasted, moaning and smiling at the flavor. Franklin opens his mouth to say something but no words come out. He just watches as she eats his flesh.

When she finishes eating, and there are only his bones left on the table, she rubs her swollen rainbow-swirled belly at him.

"That was delicious," she says to him, but Franklin can tell that she really wishes she had stopped eating his leg halfway through.

As she disposes his bones in a waxy garbage can, there is a pounding on the door.

"Pixie sticks!" she cries and runs into the bedroom with Franklin.

She hushes him, cuts him down with one of her fingernails, and stuffs him in the bed, under the covers.

"If they find you they will cut you up and feed you to the lemon hogs," she says.

She cuffs a lime brace around his neck, chaining him to the bedpost. After she tosses the covers over his head, kicks the saw under the bed, turns out the light, and shuts the bedroom door, she yells through her cookie walls at her visitor.

"Who comes here?"

"Jujube," says a man's voice. "Open now. We must speak."

The man's voice is deep and gurgling, like his throat is filled with bubbles.

Franklin, lying in the dark, hears the front door open.

"I do not want you here, Licorice," she says to her visitor.

The man lets himself in.

Franklin crawls to the edge of the bed. The mattress smells like banana and has the texture of chewed gum. He peeks his eyes out from under the rubbery sheets and realizes the bedroom door has been left open a crack.

"Float is missing," the candy man says. "We think he's dead. The passage to the upper world is filled with blood. We think a human did it."

"That's impossible," Jujy says.

The candy man paces the room and Franklin is able to get a good look at him through the cracked door. The man has black hard candy skin from top to bottom. He wears sweet tart jewelry and a tootsie roll hat. He seems to have no hair on his head, but he has a goatee made of cocoa butter.

"Not only that," Licorice continues, "but we think his murderer is down here somewhere. We found a human weapon by the soda pond."

"It is forbidden to bring human items into our world," Jujy says.

"That's why I believe a human brought it down here," Licorice says. "We also trapped some wild gum-goblins that had meat in their bellies. If the meat is that of a human then we will be able to relax, but once it is examined I believe we will discover that the meat belongs to Float. It is likely that the human killed Float and his body was then eaten by the gum-goblins. The human might still be down here somewhere."

"If there were a human down here he would have gone back to the surface by now," Jujy says.

"Not necessarily," Licorice says. "It is possible that someone found him and took him home with them."

"Who would do such a thing?" Jujy tries to laugh.

"I only know one person who would," he says. "You."

"Me?"

"If anyone would do such a thing it would be you," Licorice says. "You were always the troublemaker when we were kids. You never liked to follow the rules. You always liked to visit the human world just because you thought it was fun."

"I was a kid then," Jujy says.

Franklin sees her nervously looking at him through the door, then looking back at Licorice.

"I would never hide a human in my home," she says.

"Do you mind if I search it, then?" Licorice says.

"No, you can't," she says, stepping in front of the bedroom door.

Franklin crawls out of the covers and reaches for his cane. Because of his clouded mind, he isn't able to be as careful or as quiet as he intended. When he touches the handle of the cane, it bounces off of his fingers, slides down the wall, and makes a loud clang as it hits a chocolate chip.

"What was that?" Licorice says.

"Nothing," Jujy says. "Just my guest."

"You have a guest?"

"He's from the northern cave and needed a place to stay."

Franklin falls onto the floor. He feels along the cookie wall in the dark, trying to find his cane.

"How long has he been here?" he asks.

"He just got here today," she says.

"It seems funny that he arrives today of all days," he says. "I think I better meet him."

Licorice reaches for the door, but Jujy blocks his path.

"You can't," she says. "He's sick."

Franklin leaves the cane and crawls under the bed to hide.

"He has the cheese flu," she says. "If you go in you'll catch it."

Licorice steps away from the door. “Cheese flu? So is he going to die?”

“I’m not sure,” she says.

“How long do you plan on keeping him here?” he asks.

“At least three days.”

“Three days?” Licorice yells. “He’s not taking you as his mate, is he?”

“No,” she says.

“He better not take you as his mate,” he says.

“I’m just helping him get better.”

Franklin hears footsteps as Licorice returns to the front door.

“I will return in three days,” Licorice says, “once he is well. But let me tell you this, Jujube, if you have lied to me in any way you will be sorry.”

“I am not lying,” she says.

“Of course you are not,” he says.

They say their goodbyes and the door closes. Neither Jujy nor Franklin make a sound until the candy man’s footsteps are too far away to hear.

The light turns on. From under the bed, Franklin watches Jujy’s stiff candy cane legs cross the room. If he had his cane sword, he would have been able to stab her in the feet, knock her down, and then slash her throat right there. But his cane is too far away. She kneels down and peeks at him with her dead doll face.

“He’s gone,” she says. “It would have been a waste if they

fed all your meat to the lemon hogs."

At this range, her strawberry aroma smoothes his senses so softly that he finds himself smiling at her.

# CHAPTER ELEVEN

At night, Jujy makes him a bed on the floor and then goes to sleep. He is still chained to her bedpost. Her snores sound like she's blowing into a candy whistle.

Lying on gummy pillows and brown sugared blankets, it dawns on Franklin that he is sleeping in the same room as the monster that plagued his nightmares as a child. She's the same monster that killed Laura, Hillary, and Andrew. She's the same monster he has spent his entire life trying to find so that he could get his revenge.

He debates whether or not to kill the candy woman in her sleep. His cane is within reach. He could do it easily. Just stab her through an eye into the brain. But he's not sure if he should kill her just yet. She is protecting him from the other candy people for some reason. Franklin believes she's just hiding him like a dog would hide a bone. She obviously doesn't like the taste of him, but perhaps she feels bad about wasting any kind of food. Franklin knows she will kill him eventually, but at least she wants to keep him alive at the moment. Without her protection he's more likely to be killed by the other candy people. He wonders if it is worth taking the risk. Even if he dies, he'll at least die satisfied.

His muscles are too loose and relaxed to do anything about it tonight. His eyes droop shut and his mind drifts. Before he falls asleep, the marshmallow puppy curls up next to him. It is soft and warm against his arm. It smells so delicious that he almost takes a bite out of it in his sleep.

Franklin awakes to incredible pain. He squeezes the stump where his leg should be. The candy woman is nowhere in sight. He can't smell the strawberry fragrance. She's gone. Now that her intoxicating pheromones are nowhere in the vicinity, Franklin is sobering up. His mind is clearing and his pain is gushing in. The pain is so great that he can't even move. He screams and squeezes Jujy's tootsie roll bedpost so hard that his fingers make indentions.

The marshmallow puppy cocks its head, and watches him with black jellybean eyes as he writhes on the floor.

The candy woman returns, carrying a large white bag over her shoulder like Santa Claus. Franklin breathes her fragrance as deep as he can to calm the pain as quickly as possible. She notices him vigorously inhaling her scent and it makes her blush. The pain doesn't go away quickly enough. The fragrance just makes him dizzy at first. She sits down next to him on the floor and squeezes her toes in the air. Then she drops her bag between her candy cane legs and digs through it like Santa digging for presents.

Franklin is paralyzed at the sight of the bag. He knows what is inside of it. When Jujy pulls out a tiny hand, no bigger than a four-year-old's, Franklin figures that she has just returned from a hunt. She's killed a child and brought back the remains.

"Your teeth aren't sharp enough to tear through the meat," Jujy says. "I'll do it for you."

She rips a sliver of meat off of the tiny hand and stuffs it into Franklin's mouth. Franklin doesn't move. He is in shock. He pushes it out of his mouth with his tongue, but Jujy stuffs it back in with her long fingernail.

"You need your strength," she says. "I'm going to save you."

She pushes the meat so far back into his throat that he is forced to swallow it or choke. The meat is rough going down.

"That's good," she says.

He doesn't move at all. She begins to chew up the meat for him and spit it into his mouth. But before she makes him swallow again he sees a face staring at him from inside of the bag, peeking out among the bloody pieces of flesh. It is the face of a dead four-year-old girl, staring at him blankly as he is force-fed skin from her knuckles.

For several hours, Franklin is in a daze from the strawberry drug, from the pain, and from the shock of seeing the dead girl's face. He is only partially aware when Jujy connects a new leg to his stump.

The leg looks like that of a mannequin's only it is red and

made of hard candy. It smells like sour apple. In his daze, Franklin smiles at it.

"It matches my suit," he says with a limp smile, a line of drool slipping from his lips.

Jujy pats him on the shoulder, happy that he approves.

He is surprised when he discovers that he can move the joints and toes of his new candy leg.

Franklin remains in a drunken state for a couple of days. Jujy cuts more body parts from him and replaces them with candy parts. She removes his left hand and gives him one made of marzipan. She skins his chest and pours hot melted green apple liquid onto him. When it cools, it hardens into candy skin like hers. She cuts slits into his good arm and inserts gumballs. Then she glazes it and coats it in cinnamon. She removes his eyebrows and all of his hair. She cuts off his cheeks and his nose, replacing them with green and white swirled lollipops. She leaves his brain exposed, but decorates it with sprinkles and candy buttons.

Jujy continues to force-feed him human flesh, but he is unsure whether it is the flesh of children or pieces of his own body. He decides he'd rather not know.

Franklin keeps asking her why she is doing all of this to him, but her reply is always: "I'm saving you."

Jujy files Franklin's teeth into sharp points as she goes to the bathroom in front of him. She does not have a bathroom. She uses a candy dish for a toilet. In the middle of sharpening his teeth, she just pulled the large dish out from the corner of the room to beneath her squatting legs and began to defecate in front of Franklin as if it were the most normal thing in the world.

Blood dribbles out of Franklin's mouth. Even though most of his senses are dulled, his stripped teeth are still intensely sensitive to the grinding stone against the nerves in his teeth. Even the air brushing through his teeth as he inhales causes his eyes to water.

His senses are also not dulled to the intense aroma of the candy woman's shit piling into the candy dish like a coil of soft serve ice cream. The excrement is a swirl of pink and purple colors. It emits a very sweet and tangy smell, like Nerds watermelon-grape candy. Yet it also has a terrible stench within the sweet. A rancid infected wound smell that is far more foul than that of human feces.

Franklin cringes at the aroma and tries to break away from her grip on his jaw, but his muscles are too weak. He tries to speak to complain to her, but only blood bubbles out of his mouth. When she is finished, she pulls out a roll of toilet paper-sized bubbletape and wipes her hard strawberry buttocks. But she only pushes the candy dish to the side, doesn't even bother to put the lid back on the dish, so Franklin is forced to endure the smell through the duration of his teeth sharpening.

Eventually, Franklin builds a tolerance to Jujy's strawberry drug. It doesn't affect him as much as it did. He is able to think more clearly.

When Jujy tries to feed him the meat of a child, Franklin has the willpower to resist.

"I won't eat that," he says with his new green gummy lips.

"But I hunted it for you," she says.

"I can't eat children," he says. "It's terrible."

"No, these are really good ones," she says, looking in her bag for a good piece. "Just try a bite."

Franklin grabs her with his marzipan hand. "No, I mean it is a terrible thing to eat children. I won't eat them."

"But what will you eat?" she asks.

"Anything else," he says. "Candy."

"It's not healthy to eat just candy," she says. "You need meat."

"I'd rather die than eat the meat of a child," he says.

Jujy looks at him with a confused frown, as if he's offended her in some way. Franklin thinks that if anyone he should be the one who is offended. She digs through the pieces of flesh, looking for one that might be suitable for him, but Franklin just shakes his head at everything he is offered.

Jujy returns with a new bag of food for Franklin. This time it is filled with candy instead of flesh. There is a mound of chocolate that looks as if she cut it out of the side of a hill.

There are peanut butter taffy flowers. There are spicy ginger plants, jawbreaker rocks, and a dead marshmallow animal.

The animal looks like some kind of rabbit or a squirrel. It's not exactly either. Blood is leaking out of its white marshmallow fur.

"There is meat inside of it," Jujy tells him. "You can survive on these."

Franklin eats the chocolate and peanut butter taffy, but decides against the animal. The idea of bloody raw meat wrapped in marshmallow does not appeal to him. Jujy gives him an annoyed look when he doesn't eat it, like there is something terribly wrong with him.

"Why are you keeping me prisoner here?" Franklin asks.

"You're not my prisoner," she says. "You are my guest."

"Then unchain me," Franklin says, tugging on his neck brace.

"It is for your own good," she says.

"Just like removing my body parts and replacing them with candy is for my own good?" he asks.

"Yes," she says.

Then she points at the marshmallow animal. "It is also for your own good if you eat that."

Franklin cringes when he looks down on the creature. Its swollen bloody tongue dangles out of its white fluffy mouth.

"I can't eat raw meat," he says.

"Raw?" she asks. "What is raw?"

"Uncooked," he says.

"Like the way cookies are cooked?" she asks. "Cooked meat would be weird."

"That's how humans eat meat."

"We use cooking to make our buildings and furniture. We don't cook food. That would be gross."

"I thought you people read books about humans," he says. "You should know humans cook their food."

"I never read books," she says. "Reading is boring."

Then she smiles at Franklin and bites the marshmallow animal's head off.

# CHAPTER TWELVE

Licorice returns to meet Jujy's guest as he had promised.

Most of Franklin's skin is now coated in candy parts. He looks just like a candy man. He can't believe he has become like one of the creatures he fears. His eyes are the only thing that appear to be human. Jujy gives him a pair of green candy sunglasses to cover them.

He still wears his apple-red suit, but it has been saturated in sugar and artificial flavorings so that it appears to be candy clothes. He holds his cane in his hand, so that he can draw the sword in case of defense. Jujy doesn't release him from his chain and collar. She ignores him when he tells her it might look suspicious.

"Black Licorice," Jujy announces as the candy man enters her home.

She points at Franklin. "This is Sour Apple."

"Good to meet you, Apple," he says in his deep bubbling voice. "I hope you are feeling better."

Licorice steps forward and shakes Franklin's hand.

"Yes," Franklin says, holding the man's hard black fingers in his soft marzipan palm.

By the way the man squeezes his hand, Franklin can tell he

is making sure the hand is made of candy.

"You are from the northern cave?" he asks.

"Yes, he is," Jujy says.

"I'm good friends with someone who recently moved here from the north cave," Licorice says. "His name is Red Vine. Do you know him?"

"Never heard of him," Franklin says.

"That's funny you've never met given the number who live there," he says. "How many of them are there, again? Twenty?"

"A little more," Franklin says, putting on his best bluffing poker face.

"With such a small population, I would think that you would know everyone there. My buddy Red Vine says he knows everyone there. Perhaps you know him by his nickname, Razzleberry?"

Franklin can tell what he's trying to do. Even without his advanced brain, he would be able to see through this game he is playing.

"Never heard of him," Franklin says. "Are you sure he is from the north cave?"

"I am positive," he says. "Perhaps you know each other and don't even know it. Maybe I should introduce you. Would you like that?"

"There wouldn't be any point," Franklin says.

"Why not?" says the candy man.

"Because there's no such person," Franklin says. "I don't see the point in meeting someone that doesn't exist."

Black Licorice smiles.

"You're not as dim as Jujube," he says. "No, you're actually pretty smart. Almost as smart as a human."

"Smarter," Franklin says.

"Smarter?" Licorice laughs, and rubs Franklin's shoulder. "I think I like you, Apple. You've got strength of character."

"Thank you," he says.

"I suspected you to be the human being who killed Float," he says. "I see now that I was wrong."

"Jujy told me about this," Franklin says. "You found meat within a gum-goblin. Did it turn out to be your friend's or a human's?"

"Funny you should mention it," he says. "The meat in the original gum-goblins we found was definitely from Float. But yesterday we found more gum-goblins containing meat. The meat from these turned out to be from a human. He found a human hand in one, a human leg bone in another, a collection of human skin in another."

"Sounds like the gum-goblins got him first," Franklin says.

"Yes, it appears so," Licorice says.

"I think you better get going," Jujy tells Licorice.

"But I've only just arrived, my love," Licorice says.

Licorice pushes her aside to continue his man-to-man discussion with Franklin.

"So, Apple," he says. "Now that you are all better, where will you be staying?"

Jujy bursts between the two men.

"He's staying with me," Jujy says.

"But it's been three days," Licorice says. "A male and a female cannot live together for more than three days unless they are mates."

Jujy lifts the collar on Franklin's neck and shakes the chain. Licorice looks at the chain as if he hadn't realized it before. His eyes scan the length of the chain all the way into the bedroom.

"What?" Licorice's black ball eyes curl at Jujy. "He's your mate? You told me—"

"I told you that he wasn't claiming me as his mate," Jujy

says. "He's not. I'm claiming him as my mate."

Franklin looks at her with just as surprised a face as Licorice.

"But you knew I was going to claim you as my mate," he says. "You knew about the plans I was making for our future."

"It's too late," Jujy says, a satisfied smile on her face. "I've already chained him to my bedpost."

Licorice pushes Franklin out of the way and peeks into the bedroom to make sure the chain is actually connected to the bedpost. Then he punches a hole in the cookie wall.

"Females don't claim their mates," he says. "It is males who do the claiming."

"My mother claimed her mate," she says. "There is no law against it."

"I will not allow it," he says.

"There is nothing you can do now," she says. "You must leave."

"I will not allow it," he says.

"Leave," she says, pointing at the door.

Licorice bursts through the front door and turns back to give them both an evil glare.

"This coupling will not last," he says. "I promise you that."

After Licorice is gone, Jujy rubs her fingers through her pink hair and closes her eyelids. Franklin stares at the candy woman. Her eyelids are so white they look like eggshells when closed. He realizes that he isn't afraid of her anymore. He still hates her. He still plans to kill her. But he isn't afraid of her.

When she opens her eyes, she sees him looking at her and blushes.

"We'll have to pretend to be mates," she says. "It is the only way you can stay here. In our culture, men and women only share a home while mating."

"I don't want to be your mate," Franklin says.

His words throw her off balance, as if she has never considered the possibility of a man not wanting her as a mate.

"You don't have a choice," she says. "I chose you as my mate. You don't have a say in the matter."

"I believe I do," he says.

"In our culture, when you want to mate with somebody all you have to do is chain that person to your bedpost. It is usually against the person's will. All it takes is a little cunning, some persuasion, or physical force."

"That is why you did this to me?" Franklin says. "You wanted me to be your mate?"

"In our couplings, there is a dominant and a submissive. Females are usually the submissives, but I wanted to be a dominant like my mother was with her mate. In this cave, there are no males weak enough for me to dominate. If I did not find you Licorice would have claimed me as his mate."

"You did this to me so that you wouldn't have to marry Licorice?"

She cocks her head at the word marry.

"It is against the law for one to claim a mate who is already coupled," she says. "He will not be allowed to even try to claim me as long as I have you chained to my bed."

"So how long must I stay here?" he asks.

She dodges the question. "I'm happy that it has worked out so far. Licorice has a horrible flavor. I could not bear to mate with him. He has spent the last year building a large house for us. He wanted it to be the most luxurious house in the cave. It is being made of the most exquisite truffles, pastries, and candied pears. In the backyard, he plans to put in a dulce de leche fountain and a large gelato playground for the dozens of children he wanted me to produce."

She scratches her fingernails along her candy cane knee when she speaks about Licorice, causing a shrilling noise in Franklin's ear hole.

"I can't imagine how disgusting our children would be," she says. "I could never mate with a man like him."

"So you would rather mate with me?" Franklin asks.

"It will just be for show," she says. "Because you are human, I do not think it is possible for us to produce offspring."

"When will I be able to leave?" Franklin says.

Jujy's mind leaves the room before Franklin gets an answer. Her pink eyes stare off into space as she scratches white lines into the red parts of her knee.

# CHAPTER THIRTEEN

Beneath his new candy-coating, Franklin's skin becomes so itchy that it burns. He tries to inhale as much fragrance from the candy woman as possible to dull the pain, but no matter how much he ingests the itchiness will not go away. It feels as if bugs are crawling beneath his sour apple skin.

His stomach is constantly upset from eating nothing but sweets. There are nuts and dried fruits in some of the candies he eats, so he does not feel completely malnourished. But the main ingredient in his diet is sugar.

"You need meat," Jujy tells him whenever he holds his aching stomach.

"I would rather die than eat children," he tells her. It is something he repeats often.

"There has to be a way to get you to eat meat," she tells him.

Jujy attempts to cook a marshmallow rabbit she caught in the gumdrop forest. Franklin tries to explain how to cook meat, but as the dominant member of their coupling she does not allow him to help her prepare the food.

She skins the white fluff from the animal with one of her butterscotch fingernails. Franklin asks her to gut the animal, but she refuses.

"I will prepare the meat in the way I see fit," she says in her high-pitched elf voice. "It is my role as the dominant."

Her home does not have a kitchen. The closest thing she has for a kitchen is a dining room table and a rancid polka-dotted chest in the corner that is used for meat storage. She can't build a fire in the house, because her candy walls would melt at such a high temperature. She has to build a fire behind her house and cook it on a sharpened peppermint stick.

While she is outside, the marshmallow puppy snags a piece of the rabbit's skin from the corner of the table and pulls it down. Instead of eating the skin, the puppy rolls over onto it and then rubs his back against it in a snake-like wiggle.

Franklin misses Crabcake. He's worried about what has happened to her. If his wives have her they are probably not taking good enough care of the kitten. They might forget to feed her or change her litter box. They might even abuse her. It is also possible that they killed Crabcake out of spite, because Franklin always cared for the cat far more than he cared about either of them. But he tries not to accept that possibility. It is too unbearable of a thought. If he ever gets out of here he promises himself that he will get Crabcake back no matter what.

The marshmallow puppy sees Franklin crying and crawls into his lap. It looks at him with a panting tongue hanging out of the side of his mouth. When it barks it sounds more like a human impersonating a dog, like a voice actor who plays a dog in a cartoon.

"Circus Peanut likes you!" Jujy says, as she walks through the door carrying a blackened rabbit corpse.

"Circus Peanut?" Franklin says, looking at the puppy. He didn't realize it before, but the puppy does look a little bit like a circus peanut. He has a subtle orange tint with peanut-like indentions on his back.

"He's my little munchy," she says.

She takes Circus Peanut from his lap and squishes him into her bosom. Franklin watches in repulsion while she speaks baby language to the animal, making kissing noises, and revealing her gory teeth as she smiles at it.

Franklin goes to the table to inspect his meal. Aside from skinning the animal, she did nothing to prepare the meat. The head is still on it, charred eyeballs looking at him. The outside is overcooked. The inside is still slightly raw. The peppermint stick melted while it was being cooked, giving the meat a minty center.

Although it is one of the worst things he has ever tasted, he eats as much of it as he can. Jujy went through a lot of trouble to make it and he knows she will be upset if he doesn't eat it all. Halfway through, he asks himself why he cares whether he hurts her feelings or not. She is a monster and must be killed. But he continues to eat. He needs to stay on her good side, at least for now.

There is a knock at the door. It is Licorice. Jujy opens the front door a crack, but does not let him in.

"I saw smoke," Licorice says. "Somebody built a fire behind

your house. Was it you?"

"Yes," she says. "It is not against the law to build fires."

"Fire is dangerous," he says. "If a fire is too close, you could melt your skin or even your house. You shouldn't be starting fires."

"You don't have to tell me about fire," she says. "I've worked closely with fire before, in the candy mill. I know how to use it without melting my skin."

"There is no point in starting fires," he says. "Why did you need it?"

"I was cooking some meat."

"Cooking meat?" he says. "Why were you cooking meat?"

"I made it for Sour Apple," she says. "He likes his meat cooked."

"He likes his meat cooked?" Licorice rubs his black chin hair. "It is funny that he eats cooked meat in the way that humans eat cooked meat."

"There isn't a law against cooking meat," she says.

"But it is suspicious," he says. "Humans eat cooked meat. Perhaps your mate is really a human?"

"You saw him," she says. "You know he is not human."

"Perhaps he is a human in a candy disguise," he says. "You know it is against the law to associate with humans?"

"Yes," she says, "but I do not associate with humans. Did you know that it is against the law to interrupt a mating cycle?"

Licorice frowns and steps back.

"You have entered my nesting area," she says. "If I report this you will be severely punished."

"I only came because I thought it was an emergency," he says.

"But as you see it is not," she says.

"I'll be back," he says.

"If you come back I will be forced to defend my nest," she says. "It is not against the law to kill one who invades a nest."

"This won't be a nest for much longer," he says from the caramel road.

Franklin curls into a ball in his bed on the floor. He believes it is actually a doggy bed, because every night he shares it with the marshmallow puppy that sleeps against his armpit. His skinless chest beneath the candy coating burns with so much itchiness that he doesn't want to be conscious anymore. He wants to rip off his candy skin and pour rubbing alcohol all over himself to kill the bacteria that is infesting his wounds. He smiles as he envisions laying his skinless body into a tub of hot water. The thought of the peaceful warmth calms his nerves and numbs his body a little. But before the pleasant dream pulls him into sleep, a thought jerks him back into awareness. He thinks about how painful it would be to remove his candy skin. His flesh has already grown together with his sour apple coating. If he were to rip the candy from his body he would also be tearing off a thick layer of his flesh.

Franklin hopes he will get used to the intense itchiness in time. For now, he just has to survive. Once he escapes he will be able to find a doctor who will remove the candy and make him human again. He wonders if it is possible for him to look human again. He is missing limbs and much of his skin. He's not sure if doctors will be able to replace all of the parts of him that he has lost.

He wonders how he will be able to escape and bring the

body of a candy person to the police. It will be difficult enough just trying to escape. If he has a body with him it will be next to impossible. If there was night in this place he might be able to escape under the cover of darkness, but the purple lights beaming down from the ceiling of the enormous cavern never dim.

Franklin wonders if Jujy should be the candy person he brings to the police. She would be the easiest one to kill. She is the one who killed his brother and sisters and ruined his life. He knows he should kill her. But something deep inside of him becomes sad at the thought of killing the girl. Even though she murdered his family, removed pieces of his body, turned him into a monster, and keeps him as a prisoner in her home, he still doesn't like the idea of ending her life. She is not the monster he thought she would be. She is not a vicious killer. She just doesn't know any better.

He wonders if it is possible for him to bring her to the surface alive. Perhaps if he can gain her trust she will take him to the surface with her during a hunt. Then he can knock her out with his cane and bring her to the police.

As he lays there cringing he promises himself that he will gain her trust. He will get her to the surface. And he will make the world believe in the candy people. The only problem is he isn't sure whether the submissive member of a coupling is allowed to go on hunts. He doubts it. He is also worried that she won't take him on hunts because he doesn't eat the meat of children. To completely gain her trust, he will need to become one of them in every respect. Franklin understands that he is going to have to do a lot that he doesn't want to do in order to gain her trust. He isn't sure he'll be able to go through with all of it.

# CHAPTER FOURTEEN

Circus Peanut catches a Cadbury crème egg in his mouth. He brings the chocolate ball to Franklin. Franklin rolls the egg into the next room. Circus Peanut chases after it.

Franklin discovers that his itchiness isn't so bad when he keeps busy, so he plays ball with the marshmallow puppy. He kind of likes Circus Peanut. Even though he is a strange creature that looks a bit like a living cartoon, he thinks the dog is cute. Having a puppy around comforts him and makes him miss Crabcake a little less. Franklin always feels better when he is around animals.

When Jujy arrives with their food, one bag of chocolate and another bag of dead children, she has a worried look on her face. If it were a couple days ago Franklin would have ignored her, but now he needs to establish a relationship with her so that he can gain her trust.

"What's wrong?" Franklin asks, pretending to be concerned.

Jujy drops the bags onto her table, cracking one of the chocolate wafer boards. She groans in an annoyed tone. Her cotton candy hair is frizzed in the wrong direction.

"Licorice came to me in the park," she says. "He still wants to end our coupling."

"What can he do?"

"It is not against the law to end our coupling if we do not produce offspring," she says. "If we do not breed he will be able to claim me as his mate."

"What are we going to do?" he asks.

"We are going to mate," she says.

"But you said it is impossible for humans to breed with your kind?"

"We have to try," she says. "It is against the law to breed with humans so I have never heard of it being done before. It might be possible. We must try."

"But we can't actually mate," Franklin says. "If the child comes out half human they will know."

"We still must try," she says. "Otherwise you will be killed and Licorice will chain me to his bedpost. I would rather mate as a dominant to a human than as a submissive to such a horrible-tasting man."

Franklin breaks eye contact with her and pets Circus Peanut, squishing his hands into the marshmallow fur. He suddenly realizes what a big deal this is. He's going to have sex with the candy woman. It is like having sex with the boogie man. Not only that, but they will try to have children together. Franklin never wanted to have children. He is uncomfortable with the idea of having children. Now he is going to have one with the creature from his nightmares. He doesn't even know how it is possible for the candy people to have sex, since they don't have any sex organs.

"We should start in the soontime," she says, sucking on a little boy's toe.

"I won't kiss you," Franklin says.

They are sitting on the bed together. Franklin sits with his legs crossed. Jujy sits with her knees open like a frog. Both of them are awkward and not sure where to start. Franklin has always been awkward in sexual situations and Jujy admits that she has never mated before. The candy people only have sex during the coupling period and she has never been coupled before.

"Why not?" Jujy says, pouting her gummy lips at him.

Franklin forgot that he was trying to get on Jujy's good side. He knows this is a good opportunity to get her to like him. He is about to become her lover. It will surely help gain her trust. But the idea of kissing her gory, rancid mouth disturbs him.

"I'm sorry," he says, uncomfortably petting her shoulder. "I just don't want to taste the dead children in your mouth."

"I can wash out my mouth with watermelon soda," she says.

"I still think I would prefer not to," he says.

She gives him an angry look and her voice becomes firm. "I am the dominant. It doesn't matter if you dislike my taste."

Franklin nods his head. He rubs his prosthetic candy leg nervously and looks down at her crotch. He notices that she doesn't have a vagina. Her crotch is coated in red hard candy, like she is wearing strawberry jolly rancher panties. But the panties are not clothing, it is part of her skin. The males of their species are also coated in candy down there. He doesn't understand how they are able to have sex. There is a small hole at the bottom of the panties for going to the bathroom, but he doubts that can be used for sex.

"How does this work?" Franklin says. "You don't have a vagina."

She opens her knees wider and looks down at her crotch.

"It's because I'm a virgin," she says. "Only those who have mated in the past have exposed genitals."

"I still don't understand," Franklin says.

"The first time mating," she says, "partners remove each other's candy coating from their genitals. I don't have to remove yours since your genitals are already exposed, but you must remove mine."

"How?" Franklin asks. "Do I break it open?"

"No," Jujy says. "That would be painful and cause me to bleed."

"Then how?"

"Use your tongue," Jujy says. She opens her gory mouth and licks the air with her long snake tongue. "You lick the candy down until the genitals are exposed."

"It's under your candy?"

Jujy nods her head. Franklin looks down at her smooth red crotch. She widens her knees a little more. Franklin now recognizes that she has been sitting in this position so that he would have easy access for licking. Franklin doesn't move or speak for a few awkward moments.

"It's good," Jujy says. "It's strawberry. It's not a gross flavor like black licorice."

Franklin looks her in her pink eyes for a minute, then breaks eye contact. Although his mind is still a bit foggy and intoxicated, every once in a while he has a moment of clarity and realizes this is really going to happen. He is actually going to have sex with this monster from his youth.

"It takes a while to lick through it all," she says. "You should start now."

Franklin nods his head. As he leans closer to her, he can tell that she is releasing a lot more of her intoxicating strawberry scent than usual. It's coming from between her candy cane legs.

"Your smell is making me dizzy," he says.

She smiles. "Do you like it?"

Franklin nods his head sluggishly. "What is it?"

"It attracts mates and food," she says. "It is at its strongest when mating."

Franklin's mind becomes more drugged than the first time he met Jujy. He forgets that she is a monster. She just looks like an ordinary girl to him now, who is wearing some kind of clownish Halloween costume. He actually becomes attracted to her. It reminds him of the time he was in college and slept with an overweight girl when he was drunk. In his intoxicated state, he saw an incredibly attractive girl hiding under all the pounds of fat. He wanted to have sex with that hidden girl. As he examines Jujy in his drunken state, he sees an incredibly attractive woman hiding under a Halloween costume made of candy. He wants to have sex with that hidden woman.

Tired of waiting, Jujy guides his face between her legs. When he presses his tongue against her candy shell, Jujy shivers. Franklin licks her lollipop panties up and down. He realizes that they aren't just strawberry flavored, they are strawberry-kiwi flavored. He also realizes that her strawberry pheromones are highly concentrated in the candy he is licking.

As he licks, Franklin can feel the candy woman's pink eyes glaring down at him. He can feel her mouth widening, exposing her pointed teeth as she salivates. The more candy Franklin licks away, the heavier Jujy's breaths become. She shivers more intensely, out of nervousness and anticipation. Franklin can tell she is nervous because she is scratching lines into his sour apple coating in the way that she does whenever she's tense.

Before all of the candy is licked away, Franklin can tell that she doesn't have a normal human vagina. The skin beneath the candy is as white as paper. Her vaginal lips are puffy and hairless. The texture is soft but strong, like a mixture of marshmallow, powdered sugar, and human flesh. As the candy is licked away, Franklin finds himself giving the woman oral sex. His tongue weaves through the marshmallow folds, as she curls her claws into the back of his neck. The fluids inside are thick like strawberry jelly.

"Do you like my taste?" she asks.

Franklin nods his head between her legs.

Jujy wraps her palm around Franklin's exposed brain and pulls him away from her vagina up to her mouth. She sucks his tongue between her plump gummy cherry-flavored lips. Then she pulls him by the chain, tugging him by the collar to force him down onto the bed. As his penis enters her marshmallow vagina, Franklin marvels at how soft and fluffy it feels inside of her.

They have sex several times a day for the next few days. Jujy still has him lick her crotch before they have sex, even though her vagina lacks the candy shielding.

"I don't care that the candy is already gone," she tells Franklin. "You have to lick it anyway."

Franklin doesn't keep his eyes open when she fucks him. He can't handle the sight of her face peering down at him with her wide open mouth. The weight of her hard candy body slamming against him has created bruises underneath his tangy apple skin. It is becoming more and more painful for him to have sex. Besides the bruises, the wounds under his candy shell are becoming more and more infected. The itching has now become burning. The infected areas are swelling so much that his candy coating is beginning to crack.

All they do now is eat and screw. When Jujy is out on a hunt, Franklin tries to get some sleep. The worst part of Franklin's day is after they make love and Jujy forces him to cuddle with her. She wraps her body around him. His face pressed hard against her candy surface, which is sticky from all the sweating. This is the time when Franklin is able to speak to her, though. It is the time she feels closest to him, so it is the best time for him to gain her trust.

"I'd like to be able to leave the house," Franklin tells her, her blue arm wrapped around his neck like she has him in a headlock.

"You are chained to the bed," she says. "You can't go anywhere."

"I want to see more than just your home," he says. "It is hard for a human to spend time in one room."

"Being trapped in a home is the life of a submissive," she says.

"I would like to know more about your people and your people's culture. If I am to stay here for the rest of my life I will have to fit in."

Jujy tightens her grip around his neck. "You do not have to fit in. You just have to stay here in my house."

"I really want to see more of your world," Franklin says.

"No," Jujy says, squeezing not only his neck tighter with her arm, but squeezing her legs tightly around his torso. "I am the dominant. You have to be obedient to me and do what I say. Do not speak to me now."

"But I just think ..."

"Don't speak," she says. "Just do what I say."

Franklin opens his mouth to speak, but decides to remain silent. If he presses the matter any further he will get on her bad side. He just lies there on the bed and listens to her breathe. After a few moments, she loosens her grip and then curls her face into the crook of his neck. Her cotton candy hair tickles his nose and lips as she falls into a deep sleep.

# CHAPTER FIFTEEN

Franklin awakes one morning because of a tickling sensation crawling up his neck and the side of his face. He was woken up several times in his sleep because of a tickling sensation on his face, which Franklin assumed in his half-consciousness was just Jujy's cotton candy hair brushing against him during the night. But Jujy has her back to him.

Franklin wipes his face and looks down at his fingers to find six ants curled in balls on his hand. He looks around the room and spots a thick trail of black ants that flows across the floor, up the side of the bed, and under the covers.

He pulls the blanket away to discover that his chest is swarming with ants. There are dozens of them crawling all over his torso. Many of them are dead, glued to the wet sticky parts of his candy coating. Then Franklin feels the itchiness. It is more intense and irritating than ever before. He notices the trail of ants leads into the cracked area of his candy skin. He feels them crawling underneath the shell, between the candy and his skinless muscle tissue. He can see them through the green candy like it is an ant farm behind stained glass. The ants are chewing pathways through the scabby sugar cavern as if they are trying to create a new home.

Jujy wakes to Franklin screaming and frantically wiping

ants from his body. His hands hover over his candy skin urging him to rip away the candy to get to the ants, but he holds back the temptation.

"They're inside of me!" he cries.

It takes Jujy a while to realize what is happening to Franklin.

"That's unusual," Jujy says. "It's ant season already?"

"How do I get them out?" Franklin runs out of the bed and trips over his chain. When he hits the floor, the crack in his hard coating breaks open wider. It rips a gash into his flesh and a pool of blood fills the cavity beneath his candy skin and oozes out of the crack.

Jujy gets out of bed and helps Franklin to his feet.

"I'll clean them off," she says.

Jujy pulls a harness out from under the bed and then straps it to her waist. Then she unhooks his chain from her bed and attaches the end of it to the harness. The process takes some time and Jujy moves very slowly.

"What are you doing?" he cries, tugging on the chain and wiping the ants. "Hurry! Get them out of me!"

She pulls back on his chain. "You can't shower unless I do this."

"Forget about the chain!" Franklin cries.

"This is the only way I can unchain you from the bedpost and keep you as my mate," she says.

"Just hurry!" Franklin says.

As she takes him into the kitchen, Franklin grabs the doggy dish of water from the floor and pours it over his body.

"No, don't use water," Jujy cries. "You'll melt the candy."

"But aren't you going to shower them off anyway?"

"Not with water," she says.

In a cabinet, Jujy pulls out a hose that ends in a head similar to that of a hand shower unit. It does not spray water, but hot air.

"This is how you bathe?" Franklin asks.

She turns it on and uses it like a hairdryer on his skin.

"We only use water if we get muddy or have dried blood on our skin," she says, "This is much safer."

She still needs to wipe away a lot of the ants, but most of them are blown away by the hot air. She tries to get as much hot air into the crack as possible, but it doesn't remove any of the ants. Instead, she melts the candy inside with the hot air, smothering the ants in sugary goo. Then she melts the candy around the crack in his torso. The melted sour apple fills in the crack as well as his open wound. When she is done, his candy glistens as if brand new.

"We normally don't have too many problems with ants," she says. "They tend to feed on the candy vegetation and only bother you if you sleep outside. I've never seen them go under the skin."

Franklin nods his head. He can still feel ants crawling inside of him, but he isn't sure if that is because of the infection, internal bleeding, or because there are still some alive in there.

Jujy agrees to take Franklin on a walk. Since he is already chained to her waist and because he has just gone through a traumatic ordeal—although Jujy doesn't understand what all the fuss is about—he is able to persuade her into taking him outside of the house for a while.

"We'll go into outsider territory," she says. "Nobody who matters will be in that area. Licorice definitely avoids it."

"What is the outsider territory?" Franklin asks, as they step outside into Jujy's chocolate flower garden.

"It is where the undesirables live," she says. "The people who are too gross to mate with."

Franklin stops her.

"My cane ..." he says.

"What?"

"I need my cane from the house," he says. "It will help me walk."

Jujy gets it for him.

"I can't balance very well without it. Especially with my new legs."

Really, Franklin just wants to have a weapon in case he needs to defend himself against candy people.

After a few minutes of trekking through some rolling cupcake hills, Franklin's prosthetic candy leg becomes difficult to walk on.

"Your muscles are weak," she says

"It takes a while to get used to walking on false limbs."

"You didn't need to remove my leg," he says. "You could have just coated it in candy like the rest of my body."

"It is common for submissives to have their limbs removed during the early mating periods," she says. "It is easier to dominate one with a false leg or two."

"You did it so that I wouldn't be able to get away?"

Jujy nods. "It is also common for a dominant to want to eat pieces of their mate. Dominants claim their mates because they like the way they taste, so it is natural for a dominant to want to eat some of their mate. And most submissives enjoy watching their mate eat them."

"Enjoy it? Why?"

"It is flattering," she says. "Wouldn't you love to see your mate enjoying your flavor? Wouldn't that make you feel like you taste really good?"

"I don't care if I taste good," he says.

"But everybody wants to taste good."

"Humans don't."

"Then how do humans show their affection for each other?"

"They tell them, I guess."

"That doesn't sound very intimate."

Jujy looks at the ground and frowns, as if she feels sorry for Franklin because he's a human.

Over the next hill, they pass a small cottage. It is just big enough for one person. On the other side of the hill, they see a candy woman working in a garden, planting tootsie rolls like carrots.

"That's Minty," Jujy says. "She's one of the grossest women in the cave. Nobody would ever mate with her."

Franklin looks carefully at the woman. She is actually very attractive. She has tan skin, long yellow hair. Even though she's a candy person, she is one of the most beautiful women he has ever seen. She is far more beautiful than Jujy.

"Why do you think she is gross?" Franklin asks. "She isn't very ugly."

"Her flavor is peppermint and peanut butter." Then she sticks out her tongue as if just thinking about the flavor makes her gag.

"So?" Franklin says. "She still looks attractive. She has a good body and a cute enough face."

"Who cares about what she looks like?"

"Most people are attracted to good looks," he says. "I'm surprised she hasn't been able to find a mate."

"But nobody cares about what she looks like," she says. "Flavor is the only thing that matters."

"Are you saying a fat wrinkled woman that tastes of strawberry shortcake would be more attractive to mates than her?"

"Of course," she says. "Aren't humans the same way?"

"No," Franklin says. "Physical attraction is everything."

Jujy pulls them in a different direction before the peppermint woman notices them.

"You humans are really weird," she says.

"I'm weird?" Franklin laughs. "You have gumdrop nipples and you think I'm weird?"

Jujy laughs with Franklin, but she doesn't really seem to understand what he's laughing about.

By the end of the walk, Jujy agrees to take Franklin outside more often. She found walking and talking with him to be strangely pleasant.

"It is very unusual," Jujy says. "Most dominants and submissives do not go on walks or have conversations with each other."

"Because submissives are supposed to keep silent and do what they are told?"

"Well, yeah, but it is also because submissives and dominants rarely have anything to talk about."

While they are out on their walk, Franklin is able to memorize everything he's seen and store it within his super brain. With picture perfect clarity, he has every detail of the area they have been exploring stored in his memory cells. He knows that if he continues to go on walks with Jujy in different areas of the underground, he will eventually be able to map out the entire territory. Not only will he be able to learn the way out of this cave, but he will also be able to return to the human world with a completely accurate map of this place. He will be able to show the authorities exactly where every candy person lives, exactly where they can be attacked.

He realizes now that he doesn't need to escape right away. He is in the perfect position to work as a spy, gathering intelligence so that he can one day prove the existence of the candy people and make it possible for the military to wipe them off the face of the planet.

# CHAPTER SIXTEEN

After three straight sessions of mating, Jujy takes Franklin to a high peak overlooking the village.

"We can see the center of the village from up here," she says. "But nobody will be able to see us."

The village center is where most of the candy people live. The streets are paved with toffee bricks, the buildings are tall candy cane palaces, the gardens are well-manicured works of artwork filled with rainbow-colored flowers and chocolate statues of long dead candy sports heroes. Franklin records everything he sees into his computerized brain.

"What is that?" Franklin asks, pointing at the fanciest of buildings in the center of the square.

"That is the courthouse," Jujy says. "It is where our leaders live and make laws. I hate keeping track of all the new laws."

There is a smaller, bright banana yellow building next door to it.

"What about that one?" Franklin asks.

"That is the schoolhouse and library. I hate learning and reading books. Most of them are from the old human world."

Beyond the square, there are large buildings in the distance. Their color: coffee-ice-cream-gray. Purple smoke billows out of large chimneys and forms clouds on the ceiling of the cavern.

"What about those buildings?" Franklin asks.

"They are the candy mills. All the young people work there until they are old enough to go on hunts themselves. I hated working in the candy mill."

Closer to them, there is a field where several large candy men are playing some kind of sport. Many older candy men and younger candy women are watching from the sidelines. They are wearing pink and yellow uniforms

"What is that?" Franklin asks.

"They are playing jawbreaker ball," she says. "I hate that game. It is an obsession among the males. That is what they do for fun."

"What do the women do for fun?" Franklin asks.

"Women who have been taken as mates don't do anything for fun unless it pleases their dominant. Women who do not have mates go to jawbreaker ball games in order to attract males. They spray their scents in their direction, hoping to draw males interested in taking them as their mates."

"They want to be taken as mates?" Franklin asks.

"Most women are born to be submissives," Jujy says. "But not me. I was born to be a dominant."

"Why do most women want to be submissives? Do they enjoy being chained to bedposts?"

"Submissives don't have to enjoy anything. It is their place to obey their dominant. I would like there to be more women who are dominants, but in this cave the women are encouraged to be weak at a very young age and the men are encouraged to be strong. If they weren't influenced in this way there would be more strong women in this cave."

"Human children are influenced in a similar way," Franklin says. "Our culture influences our young to fill certain gender roles, but it is much different than your culture. Men and women are considered equals in human society."

"You mean there are an equal number of dominant women to dominant men in the human world?" Jujy asks, her eyes wide with interest.

"No, in human couplings the man and the woman are equals."

"You mean two dominants will couple? Or two submissives? What is the point of that?"

"No," Franklin says. "There are no dominants or submissives. Everyone is equal."

"But if there is no dominant who provides the food?" she asks. "If there is no submissive who looks after the babies?"

"They usually share all of the work equally," he says.

"But that's stupid," she says. "Dominants specialize in hunting. Submissives specialize in raising children. If both the dominants and submissives shared their coupling tasks neither would be very skilled at hunting or raising children. It is better to specialize. Then there will be one really good hunter and one really good child-raiser. I don't see the point in having two hunters and two child-raisers."

"The point is that the submissive would have more freedom," Franklin says. "The submissive would lead a more happy, fulfilling life. The submissives would be able to choose their own mates. The submissive would be able to make decisions themselves. They wouldn't need to submit to anyone."

"Even the weak humans choose their own mates?"

"Of course."

"But what happens if the mate you choose doesn't like your flavor?" she asks.

"Then you find a mate who does."

"But what if you don't want another mate?"

"Then there is nothing you can do about it. Kind of like

how Licorice can do nothing about taking you as his mate now that you are with me."

"It's not the same," she says. "If somebody doesn't have a mate and you want them to be your mate you should be able to take them."

"It isn't fair to that person, though. You don't think it is fair for all women to be submissives, so why do you think it is fair for anyone to be a submissive?"

"Some people are supposed to be submissives. Some people are supposed to be dominants."

"But why?"

"Because that's how it is," she says.

"But we could easily be equals," he says. "If we could be equals then anyone can be equals."

"We are not equals," she says. "I am a dominant and you are a submissive. That is how it is."

"But if you just open your mind ..."

"No," she says. "That is how it is."

# CHAPTER SEVENTEEN

The infection under Franklin's skin is getting more and more agonizing. It is like his flesh is rotting under the green candy. The swelling around his false limbs is becoming so ballooned that it feels as if the limbs are going to pop off.

The only thing that numbs the pain is giving Jujy oral sex. Every other hour, he finds himself digging his tongue between her thighs to suck out the strawberry drug. He has become addicted to it. Whenever she is away on a long hunt, Franklin goes through withdrawal. Besides the intense aches and pains, he gets emotionally unstable, paranoid, depressed, angry. He sweats and shivers in a corner. When she returns home, Franklin attacks her like a dog. He wraps his arms around her thighs and buries his nose in her crotch, inhaling the drug feverishly.

She says, "Just a moment. After I put the food away, I'll let you lick me in the bedroom."

When they are in the bedroom, Jujy has him kneel in the doorway and wait for him. She gets on the bed and spreads her legs. Then she has him crawl across the floor towards her.

The way she smiles when he licks her is more than just a smile of physical pleasure. Franklin can tell that she also smiles because she knows that he needs to lick her. He thinks she enjoys knowing that he suffers whenever he is not licking her. Sometimes she won't let him give her oral sex for a while. Franklin believes that she does this because she likes to watch him squirm. She wants him to beg her to let him do it.

When the drug seeps into Franklin's mind, he calms down. His eyelids droop shut. He lays his cheek on the soft flesh below Jujy's belly button and takes deep breaths as all the pain and stress dissipates from his flesh. These are his favorite moments of the day, until Jujy smacks him on the forehead and forces him to continue pleasuring her.

One time, after Franklin gives Jujy oral sex and lays his head on the soft place below Jujy's belly button, he notices that the flesh is much firmer than usual. It is also much more plump.

He rubs her belly and says, "What is wrong? It's hard."

Jujy looks down at it.

"What?" she says, looking down at his face between her legs.

Her belly is slowly expanding.

"It can't be ..." she says.

She rubs the swollen area with both of her hands.

"It's a baby," she says.

She looks at Franklin with a very serious, almost angry face. "I'm actually growing a baby inside me. Our coupling was successful."

Franklin watches as her belly continues to grow. "Why is your belly expanding so quickly?"

She looks down at her pregnant stomach. "Because there is a baby growing inside of me."

"But why is it growing so fast?"

"Because I'm healthy," she says. "I make sure to eat plenty of meat."

Franklin just watches her belly as she rubs herself, trying to feel the being inside of her.

Then she wraps her arms around him and kisses him gently.

"We're really going to have offspring together," she says. "Now I never have to mate with Licorice. You can be my mate forever."

Lying in bed together, the marshmallow puppy sleeping between their feet, it dawns on Franklin that he is going to have a child with the creature who killed his siblings. He wonders what the child will look like when it is born. Will it be human, candy person, or a mixture? Will its hair be blonde or pink cotton candy? Will its skin be made of human flesh or white taffy? Will its teeth be razor sharp or will Jujy have to file them to points? Franklin decides he doesn't want to think about it.

"Now that we have successfully mated," Franklin asks Jujy. "Can I be unchained from the bed?"

She moans as if he has just pulled her out of sleep.

"Now that I'm pregnant I'm allowed to let you go if I want to," she says. "But I don't want to."

"Why not?"

"I want you to stay here," she says.

"I won't leave. I just don't want to be chained up anymore."

"You can only be unchained when I'm ready for you to leave, but I don't want you to leave. Ever."

"I promise I won't leave."

"I take you out on walks," she says. "Isn't that enough for you? No dominants ever give their submissives as many freedoms as I give you. By the time this baby is born you will have to learn your place. You will stay chained so that you can care for our child while I am away. Then we will start another mating period and have another child. Then we will do it again. It is my duty as a dominant to make sure you stay in the home and take care of the offspring."

Franklin doesn't respond. He rolls over and tries to sleep. He is beginning to realize that he needs to escape as soon as he can. If he doesn't get out soon enough he will be trapped in this life Jujy has created for him until the day he dies.

# CHAPTER EIGHTEEN

Jujy is gone on a hunt and Franklin is on the floor, writhing in pain. The marshmallow puppy licks the salt from his ear as he sweats from withdrawal. The infection under the candy coating is worse than it has ever been. He reopens the crack in his torso and sticks a thin sharpened candy cane inside to scratch the itchiness. A foul odor creeps out of the hole. It is getting gangrenous. When he pulls out the candy cane, there are three dead ants stuck to it and one that is still alive.

Franklin knows that he has to get to a hospital as soon as possible or else he will die from the infection. He can't wait around for Jujy to take him on walks, mapping the rest of the cavern slowly over the course of several days. He has to find his way to the exit now. He has to free himself from his bonds and get out before Jujy gets back.

He pushes the puppy away from his face and crawls into the bedroom. He uses his cane to stand himself up. Examining the chain that is attached to the bedpost, he isn't sure how he'll be able to free himself without breaking the chain. Jujy has been able to hook him and unhook him with ease, but the chain looks as if it is molded into the bedpost. He doesn't want to break the chain because if he can't find his way out of the cave he'll need to be able to chain himself back to the bed so that Jujy won't know he was ever gone. For some reason his super brain isn't able to figure it out. He wonders if it hasn't been working properly with all the candy sprinkled on it.

After fiddling with the chain for a few minutes, unable to work it out, he decides that he doesn't have a choice but to break it and just hope he gets out of here on his first attempt. He pulls the sword out of his cane and stabs it in one of the candy links. The candy chain is much stronger than he had expected. Although not as strong as metal, it is as strong as bulletproof glass. He has to kick both of his feet against the chain as the sword cuts in the opposite direction. When the link finally snaps, the sword slams into his kneecap. If it wasn't his candy leg, it would have created a large gash.

Franklin hobbles out of the house on his cane. He isn't sure which direction to go in, but heads away from the territories he is familiar with. He knows exactly where the most populated areas of community are and doesn't want to go anywhere near them. He hopes that the exit is close to Jujy's house.

When he first entered the cavern, he was in a candy cane forest, so he goes in the direction of candy canes. Purple clouds swirl overhead as he climbs sugar frosted hills. A snake-sized gummy worm slithers across his path and hides in a bush of pixie sticks. His cane sinks into the chocolate mud when he puts his weight on it, causing his candy shell to scrape against the infected parts of his flesh.

He wanders through caramel swamplands and deserts

filled with fluffy pink cacti, following twisty trails through the many hills and valleys. Because of his upgraded brain, it is not possible for him to become lost, as long as it isn't broken. But he is realizing just how big this underground world really is. According to the area he has already mapped out in his head, this cavern is at least 15 square miles. He isn't sure he will be able to find the exit before Jujy returns.

After another mile of exploring, Franklin decides that he will give it just another hour. If he can't find the exit by then he'll have to return to Jujy's house before she realizes he is gone.

Franklin hears a scream coming from a nearby field. It is the scream of a child. Franklin decides it would be best if he ignored the scream and headed back to Jujy's house, but he finds himself moving towards the scream anyhow. He sneaks into a clearing that is filled with large piles of jelly donuts, stacked like pyramids eight feet high.

Hiding behind one of the donut stacks, Franklin sees the screaming child. He recognizes him. It is Troy, the brat from his neighborhood. He is being dragged by his hair through puddles of custard by a large candy person. Franklin snickers to himself. He thinks if any child deserves to be eaten by the candy people it is Troy.

But the smile quickly falls from his face as he sees the agonizing expression on Troy's face and sees the blood trickling down his forehead. The candy person is not just gripping the boy's hair, but his fingernails are digging through the skin on his scalp. Franklin doesn't see the little asshole who used to call him a faggot and try to kill his cat. He just sees a helpless child being dragged to his death.

Franklin steps out from behind the donut pile and approaches the boy. As he creeps up behind the candy person, he holds up his cane, ready to draw the blade and stab the man from behind. But just as he twists the crook of his cane, the candy person turns around. It is Black Licorice.

Licorice has a curious smile on his face when he sees Franklin.

"Sour Apple?" the words spill out of his lips like he is exhaling chimney smoke. "What are you doing out here?"

Franklin doesn't know how to respond. He just stands there with his cane in his hand, staring at Troy.

"Jujube no longer has you chained to her bedpost," he says. "I assume that means you are no longer her mate."

He smiles.

"Your breeding was a failure, wasn't it?" He steps closer to Franklin, dragging the boy behind him. "Very good. Now I can take her as my mate."

"No." Franklin lowers his cane so that he can lean on it. "The mating was a success."

"A success?" Licorice's smile turns into an angry frown. "Then what are you doing out of her house?"

"I—" Franklin doesn't know what to say. "She let me go."

"Let you go?"

"She no longer needs me," he says.

"She didn't want to keep you." Licorice smiles again. "That means I can take her as my mate as soon as the child is born."

"That is up to her," Franklin says.

"She won't be a dominant for much longer," Licorice says. "I'll show her that females are only meant to be submissives."

Licorice chuckles in Franklins face and turns to walk away.

Franklin drops his hand on his shoulder.

"Give me the boy," he says.

Licorice looks back at Franklin with black marble eyes. "What?"

"I want to have the boy."

"This is my prey," he says. "I hunted it. It belongs to me."

"Why is he still alive?"

"I like to eat my food while it is still screaming," Licorice says, licking his black lips at the child.

"If you give me the boy I will leave this cave and never return," Franklin says. "If you do not I will go back to Jujube and claim her as my mate."

Licorice's face becomes serious. "Sour Apple ..." He caresses Franklin's cheek with his raven-like claws. "I am curious why you want this child so much as to threaten me. It seems unfathomable that you could possibly dominate anyone, especially Jujube who obviously was able to dominate you. Submissive males are perhaps the most pathetic life form I can name, which makes your feeble threat nothing more than a curiosity to me. So I must ask you to explain yourself. Why do you want this child?"

"Because I am really hungry," Franklin says. It is the best thing he can come up with, even using his big fancy brain.

"That I do not believe," Licorice says. Then he takes the kid by the throat. "Maybe if I break its neck and watch you eat its flesh right here in front of me. Then I will have to believe you and will agree to your terms." He digs his fingernails into the boy's neck. "How does that sound?"

Franklin's eyes widen and he reaches out his hand to stop Licorice from going through with it.

"Just as I thought," Licorice says. "You don't want me to kill it. Perhaps you feel pity for this creature? Perhaps because he is one of your kind?"

Franklin considers pulling out his sword and attacking Licorice right there. He has never been a fighter. He hasn't won a fight in his life. But he might have an edge with his upgraded brain. He knows that several professional fighters upgraded their brains so that they could calculate their moves faster. It might not improve reflexes, but being able to think quickly can make a huge difference in a fight. Still, Franklin hesitates.

"It might have never happened in the past," Licorice says, "but I think it is very possible to give a human a candy disguise."

He looks carefully into Franklin's human eyes, then he says, "What do you think?"

Franklin pulls the sword out of his cane and slices it across Licorice's face, catching the candy man off guard. Although the blade was aiming for the throat, Licorice was able to avoid a fatal cut because, unlike Franklin, he does have good reflexes. Troy screams as Licorice rips his hair backwards, stepping away from his attacker.

"I knew it," Licorice says. "You were human all along." He throws Troy on the ground and points his claws at Franklin. "You were the one who killed Float."

Franklin holds his sword up, ready to defend himself.

"Now I will kill you and feed you to the lemon hogs," Licorice says. Then he attacks.

Troy runs and hides as Licorice charges at Franklin, slashing his claws wildly. Franklin isn't able to move as fast as his brain wants him to, but he is able to dodge the candy man's strikes or block them with the sheath of his cane. When Franklin slashes at Licorice, his sword does not break through the candy coating. He tries aiming for the throat, but Licorice's reflexes are too quick for him.

Frustrated by not being able to get his claws past Franklin's defenses, Licorice uses his armored body as a weapon. He charges at Franklin, forcing his chest against the side of the cane sword and shoving it backwards. The force of Licorice's slamming body knocks Franklin onto the ground. But he uses the fall to his advantage. As he hits the ground, Franklin swings the sheath of his cane sword against the side of Licorice's knee. The candy coating pops open and his kneecap crumbles like a jawbreaker broken against pavement.

Licorice folds over and shrieks with pain. With his upgraded brain working over time, Franklin calculates several strategies to defeat Licorice right there. But Franklin decides to ignore the calculations. Instead, he reacts with his emotions. All of the hate he has ever felt for the candy people fills him. His eyes burn red. His muscles tighten under his sour apple skin.

Franklin gets up and beats Licorice with the sheath of his cane. The sheath is heavy and made of metal. It feels like a thin aluminum baseball bat to Franklin, or a retractable baton. He clubs the creature in the chest repeatedly with it. Screaming in a fury. Licorice screams as his candy chest cracks open. Black powder explodes into the air with every hit. A spider web of fractures spread across his body.

Once the candy is broken apart enough, Franklin stabs his sword through the soft exposed flesh into the chocolate mud. Licorice's eyes bug out of his head at Franklin. His fingers curling around large chunks of his broken candy shell as his blood leaks out of his wound.

"I will kill you," Licorice hisses.

Then Franklin tears the blade up Licorice's torso, cutting through the shattered candy. His intestines spill out of the gash and his heart stops pumping. His black licorice head gurgles at Franklin as it droops to the side, his tootsie roll hat rolls through the chocolate mud.

# CHAPTER NINTEEN

As Franklin approaches, Troy quivers into a ball. The kid only sees another candy person.

"I'm not one of them," Franklin says. He puts his cane sword back together and then kneels down to the boy. "I'm human. I'm wearing a disguise."

Troy backs away from him.

"You know me," Franklin says. "I live in your neighborhood."

He shows him his apple red suit jacket. "You used to always make fun of my clothes."

Troy takes his pair of thick-rimmed glasses out of his pants pocket. They are cracked and bent. When he puts them on his face, his eyes light up as he recognizes Franklin behind the candy coating.

"You're the fucking old faggot that killed Jimmy!" His eyes go from fearful to enraged.

Troy charges Franklin and tackles him at the knees. Franklin's false leg twists and he tumbles to the ground. Troy punches him with tiny fists yelling "Motherfucker! Motherfucker!" with tears in his eyes.

Franklin grabs him by the wrists and tells him, "It wasn't me. I swear. It was one of them."

They look at Licorice's corpse.

"I tried to save your brother but I was too late," Franklin says. "The creature got away just as you arrived."

The boy tries to break out of Franklin's grip. "Liar! Motherfucking liar!"

"I avenged his death," Franklin says. "I followed the creature down here and killed him. I plan to kill all of the candy people."

Troy stops struggling and cries. Franklin lets him go.

"What the hell are they?" Troy says, rubbing the blood from his forehead.

"They are cannibals," Franklin says. "They eat children. This is their home."

"Where did they come from?"

"It doesn't matter," Franklin says. "We need to get out of here before any of the others show up."

Troy nods.

"Do you know the way out of here?"

Troy shakes his head.

"You don't even remember the direction you came from?"

Troy shakes his head.

Franklin lets out a puff of air. He looks around the landscape, and then turns back to the boy.

"Do you think you can help me carry that body?" Franklin asks, pointing at the corpse.

Troy nods.

"Good. Let's go."

They carry Licorice over a few hills back the way Franklin came.

When they feel safe enough, Franklin buries the body in a puddle of fudge. Then they head back to Jujy's house.

"I'm going to have to bring you back with me," Franklin tells him. "I will hide you in a place where they won't find you."

Troy stops. "I want to get out of here. Now."

"Unless you know the way out, we can't leave," Franklin says.

"I don't want to stay in this place," Troy says.

Franklin stares down at him. Troy cowers. When he sees Franklin, he still sees a candy person. There's not much of him left that resembles a human.

"I will make sure nothing happens to you," Franklin says. "I promise."

When Franklin arrives back at Jujy's house, he has no idea where to hide the boy. The house only has two rooms. Jujy would find him if he hid anywhere inside. He has to find him a place to stay outside. Searching around the outside of Jujy's house, he discovers a crawlspace that goes under the building.

"Climb down in there," Franklin says.

Troy looks at the hole leading under the house and shakes his head.

"Fuck no," Troy says. "I don't like tight spaces."

"You don't have a choice." Franklin pushes him towards the hole. "They will kill you if they find you."

The kid reluctantly crawls under the house, turns around and looks out of the hole back at Franklin.

"Not many of them come around here," Franklin says, "so you are probably safe. The one you have to worry about is the woman who lives in this house."

As Franklin points up at the house, Troy looks up and inches back into the darkness.

"She's not here now," Franklin says and the boy stops. "But if you see her you stay hidden. She will kill you if she finds you."

"Will you kill her like you killed the other one?" Troy asks.

"I don't know," Franklin says. "I need her for now. She is the one who put me in this disguise. She is keeping me safe. But I am her prisoner so I need to get back inside before she finds out I was gone."

Troy nods.

"I'll check on you when I can. If you get hungry there is chocolate and candy all around here. You can't survive on candy alone but it will be enough to keep you going for a few days. We'll get out of here soon, but I need you to stay here and keep quiet until then. Can you do it?"

Troy nods.

Franklin backs away from the hole and returns to Jujy's house. To reattach the chain to the bed, he uses the hot air from the showerhead to melt the candy chain into something soft and pliable. When he's back in the bedroom, he holds the link together until it cools down and hardens back into its original shape.

# CHAPTER TWENTY

When Jujy returns home, her belly is stretched so large that the candy on her torso is beginning to crack. She is holding her stomach, digging into her skin with her long nails. Rivers of sweat flow down her taffy skin.

She looks at Franklin with a cringing face. Franklin asks her what is wrong.

"It's coming out," she says.

Franklin goes to her. "Already?"

As Franklin helps her into the bedroom, he's able to feel her human muscles flexing beneath the sweat-drenched taffy skin. Her temperature has risen, causing her candy coating to become softer than usual. In the bedroom, she kicks the marshmallow puppy off of his doggy bed so that she can squat down over it.

"You're going to have it on the dog's bed?" Franklin asks.

"It's not a dog bed," she says. "It's a baby bed."

The candy woman spreads her legs and squats over the round mattress. She has Franklin hold her blue hand as she squeezes the baby out. Her claws cut into his wrist at the pain but she does not whimper. Franklin can tell she doesn't want to appear weak in front of him.

Her vaginal lips separate with ease in their softened state. They stretch out. Just a few inches at first, but the opening soon stretches to be a foot wide, then two feet. Franklin looks down to see something brown emerging. It isn't shaped like a baby.

"What is that?" Franklin cries.

Jujy just looks at him with an angry face.

"That's not a baby!" he says.

Jujy squeezes his hand tightly, slicing through his wrist. As his blood trickles down her blue and white arm, she tells him, "It's an egg. The baby is inside."

Once the midsection of the egg passes through the opening, her vaginal muscles squirt the rest of it out onto the doggy bed in one push. Then Jujy plops down on the mattress and sighs. She wraps her legs around the egg and has Franklin wrap his arms around her body. She lies her head on his shoulder and closes her eyes. Franklin isn't sure how such a large thing could have come out of Jujy. He also isn't sure how a chocolate egg could have endured inside of her without melting.

As she breathes deeply against his shoulder, Franklin examines the egg. It is like a giant Cadbury crème egg. He isn't sure if it is his imagination or not, but the egg seems to be pulsing. Somewhere, deep inside, is their child—A mutant offspring between himself and the candy woman who killed his siblings. Franklin doesn't know if Heaven exists. But if it does, he hopes that his brother and sisters aren't watching him right now.

After Jujy awakes from her nap, she goes into the kitchen and returns with a box of art supplies. A wide scary smile stretches across her face as she says, "I've been excited to do this ever since I was a kid."

"What?" Franklin asks.

"Now we get to decorate the egg," she says as she takes out brushes and containers of paint.

"Why decorate it?"

"It's tradition," she says.

For hours, Jujy decorates their child's egg like an enormous Easter egg. Her face is lit up like a child's as she paints pink and white swirls around the top. Franklin paints blue polka dots on top of the white swirls.

"Normally only submissives decorate the eggs," Jujy says. "But I don't see why you get to have all the fun without me."

Franklin shrugs. He doesn't paint very much of the egg because his hand is shaking. It is from withdrawal. Even though she is sitting right next to him with her legs spread apart, her intoxicating pheromones aren't affecting him. Perhaps the act of giving birth has neutralized their effects. Perhaps her body is no longer producing the drug because she no longer needs to mate.

After they are finished with the egg, Jujy leans back and smiles at her craftsmanship.

"Beautiful," she says.

Franklin feels things crawling inside of his chest. He's not sure if there are ants still alive under the candy coating or if puss is dripping out of the infected wounds. He presses his hand against his chest and pushes hard on the candy, hoping to kill any ants that might be alive in there. The pressure against the itchy wounds is painful yet strangely satisfying.

"I'm hungry," Jujy says. "Want to eat?"

Franklin shakes his head, but she disregards his response and pulls herself onto her feet. He sits there against the egg, holding his wounds. He needs to get back to the surface as soon as possible. If only he could get Jujy to show him the exit.

"Can we go on a walk today?" Franklin asks her.

"No," she says. "You can't go on walks anymore."

"Why not?" he asks.

"We're now in the incubation period of our coupling," she says. "You have to stay here and keep the egg warm."

"Keep the egg warm?"

"You are the submissive," she says. "It is your job to sit on the egg and keep it warm until it is ready to hatch."

Franklin looks at the large egg. He isn't sure how he can sit on it without it breaking.

"Do it now," she says. "Wrap your body around it while I make your food."

Franklin sits on the mattress with the egg between his legs. As he wraps his arm around the egg, the marshmallow puppy licks at the side of it.

"Like this?" Franklin asks.

Jujy pulls the puppy away from the egg and picks it up into her arms. "Yes."

Then she breaks the puppy's neck.

Franklin's jaw drops at her. "What did you do that for?"

"I'm making your food," she says.

"You're going to cook your dog?"

"It'll be easier this way," she says. "I don't have to go hunting for you now."

"But he was your pet," he says. "I thought you loved Circus Peanut?"

"I needed to get rid of it anyway," she says. "It's not good to keep animals in the house during the incubation period. They try to eat the egg."

Franklin just stares at her in shock as she walks to the kitchen, skinning her pet's marshmallow hide with her bare teeth.

For the next couple of days, Franklin sits on the egg for Jujy. She doesn't go on hunts during these days. She just watches him as he keeps her egg warm. When it is time for bed, she leaves him on the doggy mattress to sleep against the decorated shell. He's not even allowed to leave to go to the bathroom. She just holds a candy dish under his buttocks and tells him to defecate in there.

The feeling in many parts of his body has disappeared. His flesh beneath the candy coating has become so rotten it's black. He needs Jujy to leave the house so that he can sneak Troy back to the surface and get himself to a hospital. But she doesn't seem like she is going to go on another hunt any day soon. He wonders what would happen if he told her the truth. He wonders if she would let him go if she knew about his condition.

# CHAPTER TWENTY-ONE

"I have something to tell you," Franklin says to Jujy.

When Jujy looks him in the eyes, she can tell how serious it is. She crawls across the floor to Franklin and presses her body against the other side of the egg.

"I have been waiting for you to tell me this." Jujy puts Franklin's hands into hers, staring at him across the egg. "I have to tell you that I feel completely the same way."

"The same way?" Franklin says.

"Even though you are a human we can still have an emotional bonding," she says. "We can still be soul mates."

Franklin doesn't know what to say to her.

"Go on," she says. "Tell me."

"Tell you what?" Franklin says.

"Weren't you going to tell me that you submit your soul to me?" Her face becomes confused.

"No, I was going to ask ..."

Jujy bares her teeth at him and scratches her claws along the top of his false hand. "I want you to submit your soul."

"Submit my soul?"

"Yes," she says. "I've been waiting every day for you to tell me this."

"I don't understand."

Jujy groans at his ignorance. "A dominant shows a mate she loves him by capturing him and chaining him to her bedpost. The submissive usually does not love the dominant at first. It takes time for him to grow to love her. But eventually the submissive shows his love to the dominant by telling her that he submits himself completely to her. He submits his mind, body, and soul. He tells her that his entire being belongs to her and will obey her for the rest of his life. That's what I want you to say."

"But I ..."

Jujy grinds her claws deep into his good hand.

Franklin stops. He takes a deep breath. He realizes his survival depends on his response to Jujy.

"Okay," Franklin says. Jujy loosens her grip, then squeezes his hand lovingly. "Originally, I had something different to tell you. It is also important. But now that you have brought up this topic I will confess to you something that I have had on my mind ever since the first time we made love…"

He pauses to breathe, hoping Jujy is going to buy what he has to say. She smiles at him. Tears are welling up in her eyes even though he hasn't said anything yet.

"You are the most important thing in my life. You are my whole universe. You are my only reason for living. For the rest of my life, all I want to do is serve you and make you happy. I want to raise your children. I want to obey your every command." He pauses for a moment. As he notices that Jujy is buying it based on the tears rolling down her white cheek, Franklin tries to hold himself back from laughing at himself. "I submit to you entirely. I submit my mind, body, and soul. I will be yours, forever."

Then Jujy leans across the egg and kisses Franklin deeply. Her gummy lips wrap around his mouth, razor sharp teeth scraping against his teeth. He tastes dead child blood as she sucks his tongue down into her throat. Franklin has no choice but to kiss her with as much passion as he can manage.

After a while, Franklin discovers that it isn't very difficult for him to feign his love for her. He realizes that it isn't entirely an act. Although he hates everything about her as a candy person, he still has feelings for her somewhere inside of him. Whenever he looks at her, he doesn't see the woman who killed his brother and sisters anymore. He only sees Jujy.

"So what were you originally going to tell me?" Jujy asks.

Franklin takes a deep breath and reveals the cracked section of his side to her.

"Smell that," he says.

She smells his side and cringes at the foul odor issuing out of the hole. Then she licks it.

"Why do you taste so gross?" she says.

"I'm rotting," he says. "My wounds have become seriously infected. If I don't get help I am going to die."

"Die?" she says. "You can't die now."

"I'm a human. We aren't the same as you. Cutting off my skin and covering me with candy was not good for me. I need to go to a hospital. A human hospital."

"You can't go back to the humans," she says.

"If I don't go back I will die."

"What if I heal you?" she says. "I can give you new candy skin."

"There is nothing you can do. You have to let me go. Now.

I will probably die within a few days if you don't."

"You submitted your soul to me. You said you would be with me forever."

"I will come back," he says. "I promise. If I don't go I will die."

"If I unchain you then you will no longer be my submissive ... I would rather you die than not be my submissive."

"Then you can come with me," he says.

"To the humans?"

"I'll even stay on the chain," he says. "You can trust me. I have submitted my soul to you."

"What about the egg?"

"We can bring that, too."

"It is against the law to take eggs out of the cave. If anyone finds out they will feed us to the lemon hogs."

"Then we will have to make sure they never find out," he says. "So, will you take me to the hospital?"

Jujy stares down at the egg and scratches her kneecap.

"We'll have to wrap it in the blanket," she says. "And you will have to carry it."

"Okay," Franklin says. "I will keep it safe."

"If I remove your chain you have to still obey me as if chained," she says. "You submitted your soul to me so you must still do as I say."

"Yes," he says.

"We can't keep you chained because if anyone sees you on the chain they will come to investigate. Submissives also aren't allowed outside of the cavern."

Franklin nods.

After she unhooks his chain, Franklin tells her, "There is something I want to show you. Outside."

"Outside?"

"Under your house."

Jujy looks at him curiously as she wraps the egg in a blanket.

Franklin carries the egg out of the house, his cane hooked to his arm. It is difficult for him to walk without his cane, but he manages. In the back of the house, Franklin calls down to the boy.

"Troy," he says. "Come out. I'd like you to meet somebody."

The boy does not move.

"It's okay," Franklin says. "Come out."

The boy creeps out of the hole, hesitant at first. When he sees the candy woman, he cowers behind Franklin's legs.

Jujy approaches the boy and bends down to him, staring him in the face.

"This is Jujy," Franklin says.

Troy reaches out to her, timidly, to shake her hand. Jujy takes his hand, pulls him towards her and bites into his wrist. The boy shrieks as she rips a tendon out of his arm and thrashes her head like a shark.

"No!" Franklin screams, unable to stop her with the egg in his hands. "Stop!"

Jujy releases the crying child. "Why?"

"I didn't want you to eat him!"

"I thought you were giving it to me," she says. "I thought it was a present."

Franklin puts down the egg and grabs the boy's wrist. He applies pressure to the wound as he tears a strip of cloth from his apple red suit and uses it as a tourniquet.

"No, I want to take him back to the surface," Franklin says.

"It's only food," she says, reclaiming the egg from the ground. "We can't let food live after they've seen us. That's the law."

"Forget about the law," he says. "Just let this one live."

"I kill children all the time. Why do you care if this one lives or dies?"

"I know him," Franklin says. "I promised him I would take him home. Let him come with us. Please."

Jujy stares at him with an angry face. Not because he wants to save the boy, but because he is being disobedient. Then she gives up.

"I will allow this," she says, handing Franklin the egg. "But you are never to argue with me ever again. You do what I say when I say it."

Franklin nods at her and looks down to the boy.

"Keep quiet and do exactly as I say," Franklin says to him.

The boy just holds his wound, crying.

"Quiet," Jujy says, smacking the kid across the face. She turns to Franklin. "If it cries my people will hear it."

When the boy stops crying, Jujy grabs him by his wounded arm and pulls him through the yard towards the cavern exit.

# CHAPTER TWENTY-TWO

On the way out of the cave, Franklin scans the area and stores everything he sees inside of his brain. Troy whimpers at Jujy as she tugs on his wounded arm, splashing blood onto the white chocolate ground as they flee. It doesn't take them long to get to the exit.

As they go around the bend, they run into a group of candy people. The boy screams. Jujy stops so quickly that Franklin runs into her. He stumbles, but catches himself on his false leg. Though he doesn't drop the egg, the blanket falls off.

There are five candy people there. One is rainbow-colored, one is fat and red, one has a big green cotton candy beard, one is gumball blue, and one looks like he's wearing a giant wedding cake for a hat. They all stare at Jujy. They see her pulling the boy towards the exit. They see Franklin carrying the egg. It doesn't take them long to figure out what is going on.

"Run!" Jujy cries, then she takes off, going back the way they came.

Green Beard looks at his fellow candy people and they nod their heads.

Franklin runs after her as fast as he can with the egg in his arms. The candy people climb like spiders up the side of the hill towards them, trying to cut them off. The boy shrieks as Jujy rips him through the chocolate mud. Even pulling the boy, she moves three times as fast as Franklin.

"Jujy," Franklin calls, so that she knows he's falling behind.

She turns and comes back for him. Instead of running, she grabs Franklin and pulls him off of the path into the lollipop trees. They zigzag through the forest. When they get to a ditch, Jujy pulls them down to the ground.

"We have to hide," she whispers.

The candy men scurry through the forest, looking for them. Troy's cries become louder as he sees them across the pond of watermelon soda.

"Quiet," Franklin tells Troy as he holds the egg securely between his legs.

Troy continues to cry.

"You have to be quiet or they will hear us," Franklin says.

Troy continues to cry.

Jujy grabs Troy by the hair and pulls him towards her. She bites into his neck and rips muscle tissue from his throat. The boy shrieks louder.

"Jujy!" Franklin screams.

"He won't stop crying," she says. Then she bites into his throat again.

Troy stops crying. He holds his neck as he tries to push her away from him.

"Let him go," Franklin whispers. "He's stopped."

Jujy releases him. She looks at Franklin, chewing on a large piece of the boy's flesh like bubblegum.

"I'm not willing to risk our baby for it," she says.

Franklin gives Jujy the egg and goes to the boy. Blood is gushing out of him, but his jugular has not been cut. He tears another strip of cloth from his apple suit and wraps it around the boy's throat.

"Keep pressure on it," he tells the boy. "If the bleeding is stopped you will survive."

The boy puts pressure on the wound but he does not respond.

"Let's go," Jujy says.

With only one candy person in sight, they make a run for it. The fat red jawbreaker candy man is on the other side of the pond. He sees them as they run towards the exit, but he is too slow to get around the pond to cut them off. He yells for the others in a deep guttural voice.

They run into a pack of gum-goblins in the sugar grass field near the exit. The ferocious fruity-colored blobs bounce up and down at the wounded child. Carrying the egg under her arm like a big football, Jujy pulls out her red vine whip and cracks it at the creatures as they run through the field. The gum-goblins chase after them, snapping at their heels like gummy sharks.

The rainbow candy man cuts them off before they get to the exit. Jujy strikes at him with her whip, but Rainbow catches it in his purple jaws and rips it out of her hands. A gum-goblin lunges at Troy and Franklin. They duck and the blob flies over their heads at Rainbow. The candy man yells as the blob bites into his face.

"Come on," Jujy cries to the others.

As Rainbow falls to the ground, the gum-goblins swarm him like piranha. They take bites out of his candy flesh as they bounce up and down at him. Franklin looks back to see Rainbow's head disappearing into a yellow blob's stomach. The severed head still screams within the gelatinous goo.

They make it through the maze of sewers to the streets above. Hiding in a park, underneath the slide, they watch as the other candy people crawl out of the manhole after them. They gurgle at the moon and then separate, hunting the streets for the traitorous candy woman.

"Now what are we going to do?" Jujy says, almost ready to cry.

"We need to get out of the streets," Franklin says. "We can go back to my place until they give up their hunt."

"Is that far?"

"No," Franklin says.

When it looks safe, they crawl out of the playground into the shadows. Then they creep out of the neighborhood towards Franklin's apartment.

On the way, Jujy says, "I can never go back. If I return home they will kill me."

"Then you won't go back," Franklin says.

"Where will we live?"

"We can live here, in the human world," Franklin says.

"I can't live here," she says. "I would never be accepted into human society."

"Then I will hide you," Franklin says. "I will disguise you as a human as you disguised me as a candy person."

"Will it work?" Jujy asks.

"I believe so," Franklin says. "But we will have to deal with my wife. She will probably be at the apartment when we get there.

"What is a wife?"

"She is my mate."

She gets angry. "You have a human mate?"

Franklin said the wrong thing. "Not really. We are married but I do not love her. Actually, I hate her more than anyone I have ever known."

Jujy feels somewhat relieved by his words, but she's still a little angry and jealous.

"You can't have a human mate anymore," she says to him.

Franklin just nods his head.

# CHAPTER TWENTY-THREE

When they get to Franklin's apartment, Crabcake greets them at the door. The little kitty meows at Franklin and crawls up his leg into his arms.

"Crabby!" Franklin says, nuzzling his nose into his red, green, and white fur. "You're okay!"

The apartment is a bigger disaster then it has ever been. It reeks of meth smoke and urine. All of Franklin's burned belongings are still on the floor. Crabcake's kitty litter box has not been cleaned at all and the cat poop is piled so high that it has spilled out onto the carpet. Jujy puts the egg on the floor and examines it for cracks. Troy falls on the floor and crawls to the other side of the room.

Sarah, Susan, and their boyfriend, David, are passed out on the couch. When she wakes up, Susan yells, "What the fuck?"

The three of them get up. David grabs a baseball bat from the floor.

"Who the hell are you freaks?" Susan says, hiding behind David. "Get the hell out of here!"

Sarah moves in closer. "Franklin?" She examines his face. "Is that you?"

"Yeah, it's me," Franklin says.

"You have finally lost it," she says. "You've been obsessed with the candy people for so long that you've started dressing like them."

Susan looks at the bleeding child on their floor. "What the hell did you do to that kid?"

"It wasn't my fault," Franklin says.

"You're even killing kids?" Sarah says. "Are you eating them, too? You sick fuck!"

Jujy gets between Franklin and his wives.

"He's not your mate anymore," Jujy tells them. "He is mine now. We have an egg."

Sarah looks at her. "Who's this psycho bitch?"

"I'm his dominant," Jujy says. "You are never to speak to him again."

"Just get the fuck out of here, you freaks!" Susan cries.

"We can't leave," Franklin says. "We need to stay here for a while. Just for tonight."

"Fuck no!" Susan says. "You leave now."

David gets closer, his bat raised over his head. "Get the fuck out or you're fucking dead!"

Franklin pulls the sword out of his cane and points it at David.

"We can't go," he says. "Let us stay and you won't get hurt."

His wives laugh at him.

Sarah gets in his face. "You're so pathetic, Franklin. You are the biggest loser I've ever known. I married you because I thought you were going to be rich…" Then she grabs the sword out of Franklin's hand, his infected muscles too weak to prevent her from prying open his fingers. She points it at him. "But you turned out to be just a fucking joke."

As she jabs the sword at Franklin, Jujy catches her arm and throws her across the room. Susan and David gasp as Jujy reveals her razor sharp teeth to them.

"She's a real one," Susan says, trembling. "The bitch is a real candy person."

David swings his bat at Jujy, but she dodges out of the way and cuts through his neck with her butterscotch fingernails. Blood sprays onto Susan as he falls to the ground. Before Franklin can stop her, Jujy breaks Susan's neck and then lunges at Sarah as the crying young woman runs for the door. Troy watches from under the table, as Jujy rips the woman into shreds with her claws and teeth.

"He's my mate!" Jujy says, between bites. "He can't have a human wife!"

Sarah's screams echo through the apartment as the candy woman eats her alive. Jujy doesn't kill her quickly. She tears open the woman's stomach and chews her insides. She eats her way through to the woman's heart. Sarah doesn't die until the candy woman bites into her heart and tears it out of her chest.

When she is done, Jujy spits the bleeding organ onto Sarah's corpse and says, "She tastes terrible." She turns to Franklin. "How could you have mated with her?"

Jujy wraps the egg in a warm blanket that Sarah had been sleeping on. Then she presses her body against it.

"We need to get rid of these bodies," Franklin says.

"I don't want to eat them," Jujy says.

"No," Franklin says. "There's no time. We have to get rid of them."

"Put them outside," Jujy says.

"I'll take care of it," Franklin says.

He puts their bodies into garbage bags and throws them out of the window into the alley.

"I need to go down there and hide them," Franklin says.

"I should be doing that and you should be sitting on the egg," Jujy says.

"This is my world," Franklin says. "I know it better than you."

Jujy looks away from him.

Franklin peeks at Troy under the kitchen table. "I'll be right back, Troy. Then we'll go to a hospital."

Troy shakes his head.

"Don't worry. You'll be fine."

Troy holds his neck and says, "I wanna go home."

"You'll go home soon," Franklin says.

Before he leaves, Franklin plugs a flash drive into his brain and copies all of the information on the candy people to it. He puts it into his suit pocket, then turns to the boy.

"Just in case something happens to me," he tells Troy, patting his pocket.

The boy nods.

Franklin drags the bodies down the alley to the dumpsters one at a time. As he pushes the last one up into the garbage, he hears footsteps coming up behind him. The smell of artificial banana flavoring fills the air.

When Franklin turns around, he sees three candy people approaching him. Green Beard, Blue Gumball, and Wedding Cake Head.

"Where is she?" Blue Gumball asks Franklin.

Franklin doesn't respond.

"Where is your dominant?" says Wedding Cake head. "Where is Jujube?"

"Submissives aren't allowed to leave the cave," Green Beard says. "Why are you out here? Surely, it is not to hunt."

Franklin looks around the dumpster, searching for something he could use as a weapon.

"Who are you?" Green Beard says. "I do not recognize you."

"I am Sour Apple," Franklin says.

"You're the one Black Licorice was speaking of," Green Beard says. "You're the one he suspected to be human."

"The human who killed Float," says Wedding Cake Head.

They move in closer. Franklin steps back.

"You are human, aren't you?" Green Beard says. "That is why you came here. You were returning home."

"That's not true," Franklin says.

"Don't deny it," Green Beard says.

"We can smell the human behind the candy," says Wedding Cake Head.

Franklin spots what looks to be a shotgun behind the dumpster. He examines it a little closer and it really is a shotgun. He thinks it can't be possible. Why would there be a shotgun behind a dumpster? But then he thinks of reasons for a shotgun to be there. Maybe a teenager bought a shotgun and hid it here so his parents wouldn't find out. Maybe a criminal stashed it here while running from the cops. Maybe a bitter wife found her husband's hidden illegal gun collection and decided to throw it out while he was at work. No matter what the case, Franklin has a shotgun. He hopes it has bullets.

"You are friends of Licorice?" Franklin asks, a little more confident now that he has a weapon nearby.

They come closer.

"You know that he is dead, right?"

They stop and look at each other.

"He has not been seen in days," Green Beard says.

"I killed him," Franklin says.

"Impossible," says Blue Gumball. "No human could kill Licorice."

"I did," he says. "And if you don't get out of here I will kill all of you."

They laugh.

Franklin goes for the shotgun. He jumps behind the dumpster and grabs it. But once he picks it up, he realizes that it is not a real shotgun. It is only a toy.

But Franklin points the toy at them as if it were real. "Stay back."

The candy men look at the toy. They either realize it is not a real weapon or have no idea what shotguns are.

"Kill him," Green Beard says.

As Blue Gumball charges at Franklin, the sound of a shotgun echoes through the alleyway. Gumball's chest explodes into Franklin's face. Franklin looks down at his toy shotgun. The shell didn't come from it.

Behind the candy people, Franklin sees a mob of people entering the alleyway. They are all candy hunters. Parents who have lost their children to the candy people and have nothing left to live for but revenge. People like Franklin.

"There they are!" the woman with the shotgun screams.

Guns are fired into the candy people. Green Beard and Wedding Cake Head turn away from Franklin and charge the crowd. The mob screams as the woman with the shotgun is cut down by Wedding Cake Head. They fire into Green Beard, but he doesn't go down quick enough. He kills three of the candy hunters before he dies.

Franklin runs from the alleyway back to his apartment. The mob disperses as Wedding Cake Head tears off an old man's leg and beats a woman to death with it.

# CHAPTER TWENTY-FOUR

When Franklin gets back to his apartment, Jujy is sitting at the kitchen table, eating a human hand. Franklin closes the door and slowly approaches her. He looks under the table to see Troy's body.

"What did you do?" Franklin asks. "Did you kill him?"

She wipes her bloody mouth with a napkin.

"The child was already dead," she says. "It bled to death."

"He was fine," Franklin says. "The bleeding had stopped. You killed him."

"It was only food," she says.

"He wasn't just food," Franklin says. "He was a human being!"

"You should eat some," she says. "You'll see it is nothing more than food."

She gets up from her chair and goes to Franklin, licking blood from her fingers.

"Now that we're living in the human world it will be so easy for me to catch prey," she says. "They live all around us."

She kisses Franklin. He tastes the gore in her mouth.

"We can start a new cave," she says. "Right here. It'll be just the two of us and our children."

Franklin turns away as she tries to kiss him again. He looks down at the telephone. It is covered in blood. He follows a trail of blood to the boy's body.

"Did he use this?" Franklin holds up the phone to Jujy.

"He was talking to it," she says.

"Shit," Franklin says. "He must have called the police or his parents. We need to get out of here now."

"We can't go," she says.

"If they find you they will kill you," Franklin says.

"I will kill them," Jujy says.

"We have to go," he says. Then he scans the floor. "Where's Crabcake?"

He doesn't see his kitty anywhere. While searching the room, he smells smoke. It is coming from the bathroom. As Franklin enters the bathroom, he finds a fire pit in the bathtub. His cat has been skewered on his cane sword and is roasting over the fire. He turns to Jujy with red watering eyes.

"I knew you wouldn't want to eat any of the child, so I cooked you this." She smiles at him, as if she did something very nice for him and is awaiting thanks.

Franklin's words choke out of this throat. "She was my pet. How could you kill her?"

"You're not allowed to have pets," she says. "We have an egg now."

When Franklin looks into her eyes, he doesn't see Jujy anymore. He sees the woman who killed his brother and sisters. He sees an evil creature who should not be allowed to live.

Franklin picks up the cane sword with his false hand and stabs

Jujy in the stomach with it.

She looks at him with a sad, confused face. Crabcake's flaming corpse is still attached to the blade as Franklin shoves it deeper inside of the candy woman.

"You're just a monster!" Franklin says. "You need to fucking die!"

Jujy watches him as he stabs deeper. "But you submitted your soul to me?"

"I'm not your submissive anymore," Franklin says.

Jujy goes from sad to angry. She grabs Franklin by the waist and throws him to the ground. She cuts into his face and armpits.

"Submit to me," she says.

Crabcake's flames begin to melt Jujy's candy skin.

"Submit," she says.

Franklin punches her in the face. He grabs her by her cotton candy hair and bites into her shoulder. He bites through the strawberry-kiwi flavoring and into the meat, chewing her flesh and swallowing. Then he takes another bite out of her.

"I'm the dominant!" she cries. "You don't eat me, I eat you!"

Jujy bites into his collarbone and peels off the skin. Every bite Franklin takes out of her, Jujy takes a bite out of him. They eat each other and cut into each other as they wrestle through the living room. The flames melt their candy coating into liquid. The sugar becomes caramelized and sticks them together.

After a while, Jujy's biting becomes licking and kissing. Franklin continues to bite her.

"Please, stop," she tells him.

Franklin doesn't stop.

"I don't want to kill you," she says. "I love you."

She kisses his cheek as he bites into her neck.

"I promise I won't eat children anymore," she says, crying.

"I can eat human food if it will make you happy. I can be the submissive and you can be the dominant if you want. Or we can be equals. We can both be dominants. I don't care. I just want to be with you."

She grabs him by the throat and forces him to kiss her.

"You love me," she says. "I know you do."

"You're a monster," Franklin says.

"What about our baby?" she says. "You're going to love our baby. I know it."

She kisses Franklin again and he kisses her back.

The door breaks in and four policemen enter with guns pointed at them.

"Get down!" the cops shout.

Jujy jumps to her feet. The flaming sword slips out of her stomach and falls on the floor.

"Get down now!" the cops shout at her.

She doesn't move.

One of the cops moves too close to the egg on the couch. Something snaps in Jujy when he sees the cop's thigh brushing past the egg. She charges him. The other cops fire at her. The bullets break through her candy coating and enter her chest. She flies backwards and hits the floor next to Franklin.

She quivers on the ground. Blood oozes out between her razor teeth.

"She's a real one," says a cop with one eyebrow. "We've got ourselves another goddamned candy person."

Jujy reaches her hands out to Franklin but he won't take it.

"Kill the other one, too," says the one-eyebrowed cop. "They're dangerous."

They point their guns at Franklin

"Don't shoot," Franklin says. He gets on his knees. "I'm not a real candy person. I've been her prisoner for weeks. She dressed me up to look like this. I'm human."

The other cops look at the cop with one eyebrow, not sure what to make of Franklin.

"I'll show you," Franklin says.

Then he peels off the green candy shell on his chest. When the rancid odor hits the room, one of the policemen runs into the hallway to puke. Another officer shoots Franklin in the stomach.

Franklin hits the ground. He looks down at his skinless chest to see that his flesh has become so infected and swollen that it looks less human than it had with the candy coating. Blood and puss drain from his bullet wound. A few ants crawl out of the hole.

"Arrest him," says the cop with one eyebrow.

Franklin is rolled over on his stomach. His skinless meat rubs against the carpeting, picking up dirt, cigarette butts, and particles of kitty litter. As the cop tries to handcuff him, his false hand pops off.

"In my pocket," Franklin says to the cop on his back. "I have all the information you'll need to kill them."

"Shut up," says the cop as he handcuffs Franklin's good arm to his ankle.

The cops stop yelling at Franklin when they hear a cracking sound. They look towards the couch and see the egg is hatching. Jujy wraps her blue hand around Franklin's arm stump.

"Look," she says. "It's hatching. Our baby is being born."

The baby arm reaches out of the Cadbury crème egg, covered in caramel sauce.

"Holy shit," says the cop with one eyebrow. "There's a kid in there."

He orders another officer to get the child out of the egg. When the policeman pulls out the baby, Franklin sees a human baby. It doesn't have cotton candy hair or taffy skin. It is completely human.

Then one of the cops says, "What the hell is wrong with its eyes?"

The other cops look at the baby.

"The eyes… They're jellybeans."

Well, perhaps not completely human.

"She's beautiful," Jujy says to Franklin as her blood pools across the floor. "Our baby is so beautiful."

Franklin's blood drains out of his chest and mixes with Jujy's. The last thing he sees before he dies are the baby's green jellybean eyes staring back at him.

## ABOUT THE AUTHOR

**Carlton Mellick III** is one of the leading authors of the bizarro fiction subgenre. Since 2001, his books have drawn an international cult following, despite the fact that they have been shunned by most libraries and chain bookstores.

He won the Wonderland Book Award for his novel, *Warrior Wolf Women of the Wasteland*, in 2009. His short fiction has appeared in *Vice Magazine, The Year's Best Fantasy and Horror #16, The Magazine of Bizarro Fiction,* and *Zombies: Encounters with the Hungry Dead*, among others. He is also a graduate of Clarion West, where he studied under the likes of Chuck Palahniuk, Connie Willis, and Cory Doctorow.

He lives in Portland, OR, the bizarro fiction mecca.

Visit him online at **www.carltonmellick.com**

# BIZARRO BOOKS

## CATALOG SPRING 2012

Your major resource for the bizarro fiction genre:

**WWW.BIZARROCENTRAL.COM**

Introduce yourselves to the bizarro fiction genre and all of its authors with the Bizarro Starter Kit series. Each volume features short novels and short stories by ten of the leading bizarro authors, designed to give you a perfect sampling of the genre for only $10.

**BB-0X1**
**"The Bizarro Starter Kit"**
**(Orange)**
Featuring D. Harlan Wilson, Carlton Mellick III, Jeremy Robert Johnson, Kevin L Donihe, Gina Ranalli, Andre Duza, Vincent W. Sakowski, Steve Beard, John Edward Lawson, and Bruce Taylor.
**236 pages   $10**

**BB-0X2**
**"The Bizarro Starter Kit"**
**(Blue)**
Featuring Ray Fracalossy, Jeremy C. Shipp, Jordan Krall, Mykle Hansen, Andersen Prunty, Eckhard Gerdes, Bradley Sands, Steve Aylett, Christian TeBordo, and Tony Rauch. **244 pages   $10**

**BB-0X2**
**"The Bizarro Starter Kit"**
**(Purple)**
Featuring Russell Edson, Athena Villaverde, David Agranoff, Matthew Revert, Andrew Goldfarb, Jeff Burk, Garrett Cook, Kris Saknussemm, Cody Goodfellow, and Cameron Pierce **264 pages $10**

BB-001 **"The Kafka Effekt" D. Harlan Wilson** — A collection of forty-four irreal short stories loosely written in the vein of Franz Kafka, with more than a pinch of William S. Burroughs sprinkled on top. **211 pages $14**

BB-002 **"Satan Burger" Carlton Mellick III** — The cult novel that put Carlton Mellick III on the map ... Six punks get jobs at a fast food restaurant owned by the devil in a city violently overpopulated by surreal alien cultures. **236 pages $14**

BB-003 **"Some Things Are Better Left Unplugged" Vincent Sakwoski** — Join The Man and his Nemesis, the obese tabby, for a nightmare roller coaster ride into this postmodern fantasy. **152 pages $10**

BB-004 **"Shall We Gather At the Garden?" Kevin L Donihe** — Donihe's Debut novel. Midgets take over the world, The Church of Lionel Richie vs. The Church of the Byrds, plant porn and more! **244 pages $14**

BB-005 **"Razor Wire Pubic Hair" Carlton Mellick III** — A genderless humandildo is purchased by a razor dominatrix and brought into her nightmarish world of bizarre sex and mutilation. **176 pages $11**

BB-006 **"Stranger on the Loose" D. Harlan Wilson** — The fiction of Wilson's 2nd collection is planted in the soil of normalcy, but what grows out of that soil is a dark, witty, otherworldly jungle... **228 pages $14**

BB-007 **"The Baby Jesus Butt Plug" Carlton Mellick III** — Using clones of the Baby Jesus for anal sex will be the hip sex fetish of the future. **92 pages $10**

BB-008 **"Fishyfleshed" Carlton Mellick III** — The world of the past is an illogical flatland lacking in dimension and color, a sick-scape of crispy squid people wandering the desert for no apparent reason. **260 pages $14**

BB-009 **"Dead Bitch Army" Andre Duza** — Step into a world filled with racist teenagers, cannibals, 100 warped Uncle Sams, automobiles with razor-sharp teeth, living graffiti, and a pissed-off zombie bitch out for revenge. **344 pages $16**

BB-010 **"The Menstruating Mall" Carlton Mellick III** — "The Breakfast Club meets Chopping Mall as directed by David Lynch." - Brian Keene **212 pages $12**

BB-011 **"Angel Dust Apocalypse" Jeremy Robert Johnson** — Meth-heads, man-made monsters, and murderous Neo-Nazis. "Seriously amazing short stories..." - Chuck Palahniuk, author of Fight Club **184 pages $11**

BB-012 **"Ocean of Lard" Kevin L Donihe / Carlton Mellick III** — A parody of those old Choose Your Own Adventure kid's books about some very odd pirates sailing on a sea made of animal fat. **176 pages $12**

BB-015 **"Foop!" Chris Genoa** — Strange happenings are going on at Dactyl, Inc, the world's first and only time travel tourism company.
"A surreal pie in the face!" - Christopher Moore **300 pages $14**

**BB-020 "Punk Land" Carlton Mellick III** — In the punk version of Heaven, the anarchist utopia is threatened by corporate fascism and only Goblin, Mortician's sperm, and a blue-mohawked female assassin named Shark Girl can stop them. **284 pages $15**

BB-027 **"Siren Promised" Jeremy Robert Johnson & Alan M Clark** — Nominated for the Bram Stoker Award. A potent mix of bad drugs, bad dreams, brutal bad guys, and surreal/incredible art by Alan M. Clark. **190 pages $13**

BB-031**"Sea of the Patchwork Cats" Carlton Mellick III** — A quiet dreamlike tale set in the ashes of the human race. For Mellick enthusiasts who also adore The Twilight Zone. **112 pages $10**

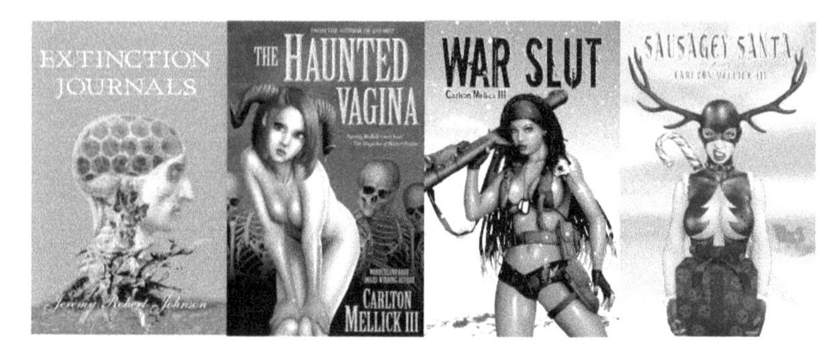


BB-032 **"Extinction Journals" Jeremy Robert Johnson** — An uncanny voyage across a newly nuclear America where one man must confront the problems associated with loneliness, insane dieties, radiation, love, and an ever-evolving cockroach suit with a mind of its own. **104 pages $10**

BB-037 **"The Haunted Vagina" Carlton Mellick III** — It's difficult to love a woman whose vagina is a gateway to the world of the dead. **132 pages $10**

BB-043 **"War Slut" Carlton Mellick III** — Part "1984," part "Waiting for Godot," and part action horror video game adaptation of John Carpenter's "The Thing." **116 pages $10**

BB-047 **"Sausagey Santa" Carlton Mellick III** — A bizarro Christmas tale featuring Santa as a piratey mutant with a body made of sausages. 124 pages $10

BB-048 **"Misadventures in a Thumbnail Universe" Vincent Sakowski** — Dive deep into the surreal and satirical realms of neo-classical Blender Fiction, filled with television shoes and flesh-filled skies. **120 pages $10**

BB-053 **"Ballad of a Slow Poisoner" Andrew Goldfarb** — Millford Mutterwurst sat down on a Tuesday to take his afternoon tea, and made the unpleasant discovery that his elbows were becoming flatter. **128 pages $10**

BB-055 **"Help! A Bear is Eating Me" Mykle Hansen** — The bizarro, heart-warming, magical tale of poor planning, hubris and severe blood loss...
**150 pages $11**

BB-056 **"Piecemeal June" Jordan Krall** — A man falls in love with a living sex doll, but with love comes danger when her creator comes after her with crab-squid assassins. **90 pages $9**

BB-058 **"The Overwhelming Urge" Andersen Prunty** — A collection of bizarro tales by Andersen Prunty. **150 pages $11**

BB-059 **"Adolf in Wonderland" Carlton Mellick III** — A dreamlike adventure that takes a young descendant of Adolf Hitler's design and sends him down the rabbit hole into a world of imperfection and disorder. **180 pages $11**

BB-061 **"Ultra Fuckers" Carlton Mellick III** — Absurdist suburban horror about a couple who enter an upper middle class gated community but can't find their way out. **108 pages $9**

BB-062 **"House of Houses" Kevin L. Donihe** — An odd man wants to marry his house. Unfortunately, all of the houses in the world collapse at the same time in the Great House Holocaust. Now he must travel to House Heaven to find his departed fiancee. **172 pages $11**

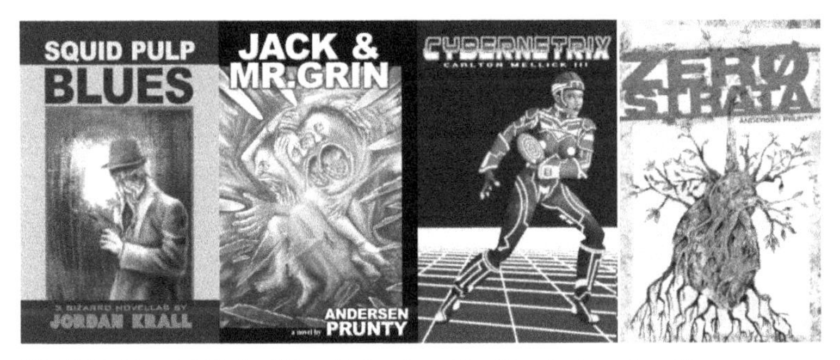


BB-064 **"Squid Pulp Blues" Jordan Krall** — In these three bizarro-noir novellas, the reader is thrown into a world of murderers, drugs made from squid parts, deformed gun-toting veterans, and a mischievous apocalyptic donkey. **204 pages $12**

BB-065 **"Jack and Mr. Grin" Andersen Prunty** — "When Mr. Grin calls you can hear a smile in his voice. Not a warm and friendly smile, but the kind that seizes your spine in fear. You don't need to pay your phone bill to hear it. That smile is in every line of Prunty's prose." - Tom Bradley. **208 pages $12**

BB-066 **"Cybernetrix" Carlton Mellick III** — What would you do if your normal everyday world was slowly mutating into the video game world from Tron? **212 pages $12**

BB-072 **"Zerostrata" Andersen Prunty** — Hansel Nothing lives in a tree house, suffers from memory loss, has a very eccentric family, and falls in love with a woman who runs naked through the woods every night. **144 pages $11**

BB-073 **"The Egg Man" Carlton Mellick III** — It is a world where humans reproduce like insects. Children are the property of corporations, and having an enormous ten-foot brain implanted into your skull is a grotesque sexual fetish. Mellick's industrial urban dystopia is one of his darkest and grittiest to date. **184 pages $11**

BB-074 **"Shark Hunting in Paradise Garden" Cameron Pierce** — A group of strange humanoid religious fanatics travel back in time to the Garden of Eden to discover it is invested with hundreds of giant flying maneating sharks. **150 pages $10**

BB-075 **"Apeshit" Carlton Mellick III -** Friday the 13th meets Visitor Q. Six hipster teens go to a cabin in the woods inhabited by a deformed killer. An incredibly fucked-up parody of B-horror movies with a bizarro slant. **192 pages $12**

BB-076 **"Fuckers of Everything on the Crazy Shitting Planet of the Vomit At smosphere" Mykle Hansen -** Three bizarro satires. Monster Cocks, Journey to the Center of Agnes Cuddlebottom, and Crazy Shitting Planet. **228 pages $12**

BB-077 **"The Kissing Bug" Daniel Scott Buck** — In the tradition of Roald Dahl, Tim Burton, and Edward Gorey, comes this bizarro anti-war children's story about a bohemian conenose kissing bug who falls in love with a human woman. **116 pages $10**

BB-078 **"MachoPoni" Lotus Rose** — It's My Little Pony... *Bizarro* style! A long time ago Poniworld was split in two. On one side of the Jagged Line is the Pastel Kingdom, a magical land of music, parties, and positivity. On the other side of the Jagged Line is Dark Kingdom inhabited by an army of undead ponies. **148 pages $11**

BB-079 **"The Faggiest Vampire" Carlton Mellick III** — A Roald Dahl-esque children's story about two faggy vampires who partake in a mustache competition to find out which one is truly the faggiest. **104 pages $10**

BB-080 **"Sky Tongues" Gina Ranalli** — The autobiography of Sky Tongues, the biracial hermaphrodite actress with tongues for fingers. Follow her strange life story as she rises from freak to fame. **204 pages $12**

BB-081 **"Washer Mouth" Kevin L. Donihe** - A washing machine becomes human and pursues his dream of meeting his favorite soap opera star. **244 pages $11**

BB-082 **"Shatnerquake" Jeff Burk** - All of the characters ever played by William Shatner are suddenly sucked into our world. Their mission: hunt down and destroy the real William Shatner. **100 pages $10**

BB-083 **"The Cannibals of Candyland" Carlton Mellick III** - There exists a race of cannibals that are made of candy. They live in an underground world made out of candy. One man has dedicated his life to killing them all. **170 pages $11**

BB-084 **"Slub Glub in the Weird World of the Weeping Willows" Andrew Goldfarb** - The charming tale of a blue glob named Slub Glub who helps the weeping willows whose tears are flooding the earth. There are also hyenas, ghosts, and a voodoo priest **100 pages $10**

BB-085 **"Super Fetus" Adam Pepper** - Try to abort this fetus and he'll kick your ass! **104 pages $10**

BB-086 **"Fistful of Feet" Jordan Krall** - A bizarro tribute to spaghetti westerns, featuring Cthulhu-worshipping Indians, a woman with four feet, a crazed gunman who is obsessed with sucking on candy, Syphilis-ridden mutants, sexually transmitted tattoos, and a house devoted to the freakiest fetishes. **228 pages $12**

BB-087 **"Ass Goblins of Auschwitz" Cameron Pierce** - It's Monty Python meets Nazi exploitation in a surreal nightmare as can only be imagined by Bizarro author Cameron Pierce. **104 pages $10**

BB-088 **"Silent Weapons for Quiet Wars" Cody Goodfellow** - "This is high-end psychological surrealist horror meets bottom-feeding low-life crime in a techno-thrilling science fiction world full of Lovecraft and magic..." -John Skipp **212 pages $12**

**BB-089 "Warrior Wolf Women of the Wasteland" Carlton Mellick III** — Road Warrior Werewolves versus McDonaldland Mutants...post-apocalyptic fiction has never been quite like this. **316 pages $13**

**BB-091 "Super Giant Monster Time" Jeff Burk** — A tribute to choose your own adventures and Godzilla movies. Will you escape the giant monsters that are rampaging the fuck out of your city and shit? Or will you join the mob of alien-controlled punk rockers causing chaos in the streets? What happens next depends on you. **188 pages $12**

**BB-092 "Perfect Union" Cody Goodfellow** — "Cronenberg's THE FLY on a grand scale: human/insect gene-spliced body horror, where the human hive politics are as shocking as the gore." -John Skipp. **272 pages $13**

**BB-093 "Sunset with a Beard" Carlton Mellick III** — 14 stories of surreal science fiction. **200 pages $12**

**BB-094 "My Fake War" Andersen Prunty** — The absurd tale of an unlikely soldier forced to fight a war that, quite possibly, does not exist. It's Rambo meets Waiting for Godot in this subversive satire of American values and the scope of the human imagination. **128 pages $11**

**BB-095 "Lost in Cat Brain Land" Cameron Pierce** — Sad stories from a surreal world. A fascist mustache, the ghost of Franz Kafka, a desert inside a dead cat. Primordial entities mourn the death of their child. The desperate serve tea to mysterious creatures. A hopeless romantic falls in love with a pterodactyl. And much more. **152 pages $11**

**BB-096 "The Kobold Wizard's Dildo of Enlightenment +2" Carlton Mellick III** — A Dungeons and Dragons parody about a group of people who learn they are only made up characters in an AD&D campaign and must find a way to resist their nerdy teenaged players and retarded dungeon master in order to survive. 232 **pages $12**

**BB-098 "A Hundred Horrible Sorrows of Ogner Stump" Andrew Goldfarb** — Goldfarb's acclaimed comic series. A magical and weird journey into the horrors of everyday life. **164 pages $11**

BB-099 **"Pickled Apocalypse of Pancake Island" Cameron Pierce**—A demented fairy tale about a pickle, a pancake, and the apocalypse. **102 pages $8**

BB-100 **"Slag Attack" Andersen Prunty**— Slag Attack features four visceral, noir stories about the living, crawling apocalypse.A slag is what survivors are calling the slug-like maggots raining from the sky, burrowing inside people, and hollowing out their flesh and their sanity. **148 pages $11**

BB-101 **"Slaughterhouse High" Robert Devereaux**—A place where schools are built with secret passageways, rebellious teens get zippers installed in their mouths and genitals, and once a year, on that special night, one couple is slaughtered and the bits of their bodies are kept as souvenirs. **304 pages $13**

BB-102 **"The Emerald Burrito of Oz" John Skipp & Marc Levinthal** —OZ IS REAL! Magic is real! The gate is really in Kansas! And America is finally allowing Earth tourists to visit this weird-ass, mysterious land. But when Gene of Los Angeles heads off for summer vacation in the Emerald City, little does he know that a war is brewing...a war that could destroy both worlds. **280 pages $13**

BB-103 **"The Vegan Revolution... with Zombies" David Agranoff**— When there's no more meat in hell, the vegans will walk the earth. **160 pages $11**

BB-104 **"The Flappy Parts" Kevin L Donihe**—Poems about bunnies, LSD, and police abuse. You know, things that matter. 132 **pages $11**

BB-105 **"Sorry I Ruined Your Orgy" Bradley Sands**—Bizarro humorist Bradley Sands returns with one of the strangest, most hilarious collections of the year. **130 pages $11**

BB-106 **"Mr. Magic Realism" Bruce Taylor**—Like Golden Age science fiction comics written by Freud, *Mr. Magic Realism* is a strange, insightful adventure that spans the furthest reaches of the galaxy, exploring the hidden caverns in the hearts and minds of men, women, aliens, and biomechanical cats. **152 pages $11**

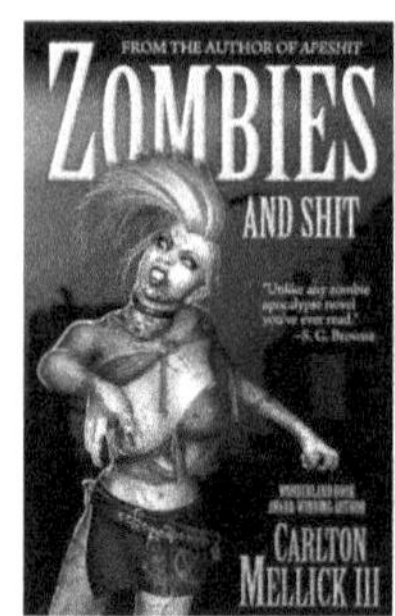

BB-107 **"Zombies and Shit" Carlton Mellick III**—"Battle Royale" meets "Return of the Living Dead." Mellick's bizarro tribute to the zombie genre. **308 pages $13**

BB-108 **"The Cannibal's Guide to Ethical Living" Mykle Hansen**—Over a five star French meal of fine wine, organic vegetables and human flesh, a lunatic delivers a witty, chilling, disturbingly sane argument in favor of eating the rich.. **184 pages $11**

BB-109 **"Starfish Girl" Athena Villaverde**—In a post-apocalyptic underwater dome society, a girl with a starfish growing from her head and an assassin with sea anemone hair are on the run from a gang of mutant fish men. **160 pages $11**

BB-110 **"Lick Your Neighbor" Chris Genoa**—Mutant ninjas, a talking whale, kung fu masters, maniacal pilgrims, and an alcoholic clown populate Chris Genoa's surreal, darkly comical and unnerving reimagining of the first Thanksgiving. **303 pages $13**

BB-111 **"Night of the Assholes" Kevin L. Donihe**—A plague of assholes is infecting the countryside. Normal everyday people are transforming into jerks, snobs, dicks, and douchebags. And they all have only one purpose: to make your life a living hell.. **192 pages $11**

BB-112 **"Jimmy Plush, Teddy Bear Detective" Garrett Cook**—Hard-boiled cases of a private detective trapped within a teddy bear body. **180 pages $11**

BB-113 **"The Deadheart Shelters" Forrest Armstrong**—The hip hop lovechild of William Burroughs and Dali... **144 pages $11**

BB-114 **"Eyeballs Growing All Over Me... Again" Tony Raugh**—Absurd, surreal, playful, dream-like, whimsical, and a lot of fun to read. **144 pages $11**

BB-115 **"Whargoul" Dave Brockie** — From the killing grounds of Stalingrad to the death camps of the holocaust. From torture chambers in Iraq to race riots in the United States, the Whargoul was there, killing and raping. **244 pages $12**

BB-116 **"By the Time We Leave Here, We'll Be Friends" J. David Osborne** — A David Lynchian nightmare set in a Russian gulag, where its prisoners, guards, traitors, soldiers, lovers, and demons fight for survival and their own rapidly deteriorating humanity. **168 pages $11**

BB-117 **"Christmas on Crack" edited by Carlton Mellick III** — Perverted Christmas Tales for the whole family! . . . as long as every member of your family is over the age of 18. **168 pages $11**

BB-118 **"Crab Town" Carlton Mellick III** — Radiation fetishists, balloon people, mutant crabs, sail-bike road warriors, and a love affair between a woman and an H-Bomb. This is one mean asshole of a city. Welcome to Crab Town. **100 pages $8**

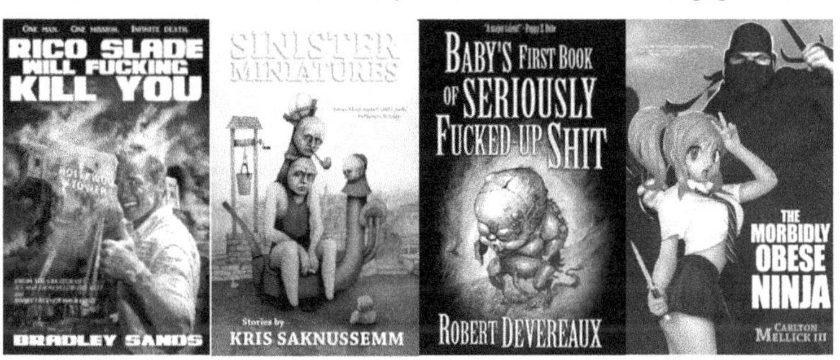


BB-119 **"Rico Slade Will Fucking Kill You" Bradley Sands** — Rico Slade is an action hero. Rico Slade can rip out a throat with his bare hands. Rico Slade's favorite food is the honey-roasted peanut. Rico Slade will fucking kill everyone. A novel. **122 pages $8**

BB-120 **"Sinister Miniatures" Kris Saknussemm** — The definitive collection of short fiction by Kris Saknussemm, confirming that he is one of the best, most daring writers of the weird to emerge in the twenty-first century. **180 pages $11**

BB-121 **"Baby's First Book of Seriously Fucked up Shit" Robert Devereaux** — Ten stories of the strange, the gross, and the just plain fucked up from one of the most original voices in horror. **176 pages $11**

BB-122 **"The Morbidly Obese Ninja" Carlton Mellick III** — These days, if you want to run a successful company . . . you're going to need a lot of ninjas. **92 pages $8**

BB-123 **"Abortion Arcade" Cameron Pierce** — An intoxicating blend of body horror and midnight movie madness, reminiscent of early David Lynch and the splatterpunks at their most sublime. **172 pages $11**

BB-124 **"Black Hole Blues" Patrick Wensink** — A hilarious double helix of country music and physics. **196 pages $11**

BB-125 **"Barbarian Beast Bitches of the Badlands" Carlton Mellick III** — Three prequels and sequels to *Warrior Wolf Women of the Wasteland.* **284 pages $13**

BB-126 **"The Traveling Dildo Salesman" Kevin L. Donihe** — A nightmare comedy about destiny, faith, and sex toys. Also featuring Donihe's most lurid and infamous short stories: *Milky Agitation, Two-Way Santa, The Helen Mower, Living Room Zombies,* and *Revenge of the Living Masturbation Rag.* **108 pages $8**

BB-127 **"Metamorphosis Blues" Bruce Taylor** — Enter a land of love beasts, intergalactic cowboys, and rock 'n roll. A land where Sears Catalogs are doorways to insanity and men keep mysterious black boxes. Welcome to the monstrous mind of Mr. Magic Realism. **136 pages $11**

BB-128 **"The Driver's Guide to Hitting Pedestrians" Andersen Prunty** — A pocket guide to the twenty-three most painful things in life, written by the most well-adjusted man in the universe. **108 pages $8**

BB-129 **"Island of the Super People" Kevin Shamel** — Four students and their anthropology professor journey to a remote island to study its indigenous population. But this is no ordinary native culture. They're super heroes and villains with flesh costumes and outlandish abilities like self-detonation, musical eyelashes, and microwave hands. **194 pages $11**

BB-130 **"Fantastic Orgy" Carlton Mellick III** — Shark Sex, mutant cats, and strange sexually transmitted diseases. Featuring the stories: *Candy-coated, Ear Cat, Fantastic Orgy, City Hobgoblins,* and *Porno in August.* **136 pages $9**

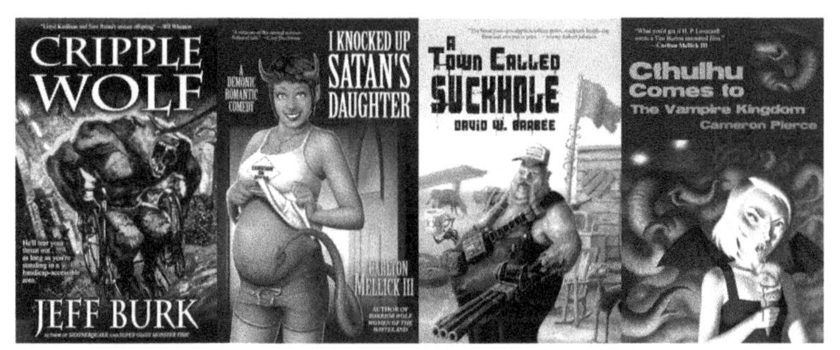


BB-131 **"Cripple Wolf" Jeff Burk** — Part man. Part wolf. 100% crippled. Also including *Punk Rock Nursing Home, Adrift with Space Badgers, Cook for Your Life, Just Another Day in the Park, Frosty and the Full Monty*, and *House of Cats.* **152 pages $10**

BB-132 **"I Knocked Up Satan's Daughter" Carlton Mellick III** — An adorable, violent, fantastical love story. A romantic comedy for the bizarro fiction reader. **152 pages $10**

BB-133 **"A Town Called Suckhole" David W. Barbee** — Far into the future, in the nuclear bowels of post-apocalyptic Dixie, there is a town. A town of derelict mobile homes, ancient junk, and mutant wildlife. A town of slack jawed rednecks who bask in the splendors of moonshine and mud boggin'. A town dedicated to the bloody and demented legacy of the Old South. A town called Suckhole. **144 pages $10**

BB-134 **"Cthulhu Comes to the Vampire Kingdom" Cameron Pierce** — What you'd get if H. P. Lovecraft wrote a Tim Burton animated film. **148 pages $11**

BB-135 **"I am Genghis Cum" Violet LeVoit** — From the savage Arctic tundra to post-partum mutations to your missing daughter's unmarked grave, join visionary madwoman Violet LeVoit in this non-stop eight-story onslaught of full-tilt Bizarro punk lit thrills. **124 pages $9**

BB-136 **"Haunt" Laura Lee Bahr** — A tripping-balls Los Angeles noir, where a mysterious dame drags you through a time-warping Bizarro hall of mirrors. **316 pages $13**

BB-137 **"Amazing Stories of the Flying Spaghetti Monster" edited by Cameron Pierce** — Like an all-spaghetti evening of Adult Swim, the Flying Spaghetti Monster will show you the many realms of His Noodly Appendage. Learn of those who worship him and the lives he touches in distant, mysterious ways. **228 pages $12**

BB-138 **"Wave of Mutilation" Douglas Lain** — A dream-pop exploration of modern architecture and the American identity, *Wave of Mutilation* is a Zen finger trap for the 21st century. **100 pages $8**

BB-139 **"Hooray for Death!" Mykle Hansen** — Famous Author Mykle Hansen draws unconventional humor from deaths tiny and large, and invites you to laugh while you can. **128 pages $10**

BB-140 **"Hypno-hog's Moonshine Monster Jamboree" Andrew Goldfarb** — Hicks, Hogs, Horror! Goldfarb is back with another strange illustrated tale of backwoods weirdness. **120 pages $9**

BB-141 **"Broken Piano For President" Patrick Wensink** — A comic masterpiece about the fast food industry, booze, and the necessity to choose happiness over work and security. **372 pages $15**

BB-142 **"Please Do Not Shoot Me in the Face" Bradley Sands** — A novel in three parts, *Please Do Not Shoot Me in the Face: A Novel,* is the story of one boy detective, the worst ninja in the world, and the great American fast food wars. It is a novel of loss, destruction, and--incredibly--genuine hope. **224 pages $12**

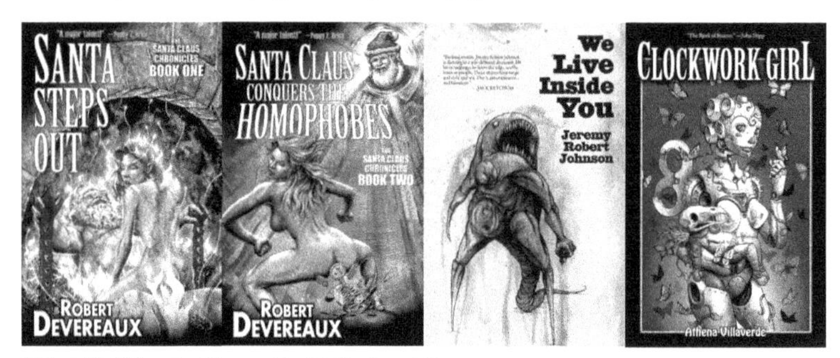


BB-143 **"Santa Steps Out" Robert Devereaux** — Sex, Death, and Santa Claus ... The ultimate erotic Christmas story is back. **294 pages $13**

BB-144 **"Santa Conquers the Homophobes" Robert Devereaux** — "I wish I could hope to ever attain one-thousandth the perversity of Robert Devereaux's toenail clippings." - Poppy Z. Brite **316 pages $13**

BB-145 **"We Live Inside You" Jeremy Robert Johnson** — "Jeremy Robert Johnson is dancing to a way different drummer. He loves language, he loves the edge, and he loves us people. These stories have range and style and wit. This is entertainment... and literature."- Jack Ketchum **188 pages $11**

BB-146 **"Clockwork Girl" Athena Villaverde** — Urban fairy tales for the weird girl in all of us. Like a combination of Francesca Lia Block, Charles de Lint, Kathe Koja, Tim Burton, and Hayao Miyazaki, her stories are cute, kinky, edgy, magical, provocative, and strange, full of poetic imagery and vicious sexuality. **160 pages $10**

BB-147 **"Armadillo Fists" Carlton Mellick III** — A weird-as-hell gangster story set in a world where people drive giant mechanical dinosaurs instead of cars. **168 pages $11**

BB-148 **"Gargoyle Girls of Spider Island" Cameron Pierce** — Four college seniors venture out into open waters for the tropical party weekend of a lifetime. Instead of a teenage sex fantasy, they find themselves in a nightmare of pirates, sharks, and sex-crazed monsters. **100 pages $8**

BB-149 **"The Handsome Squirm" by Carlton Mellick III** — Like Franz Kafka's *The Trial* meets an erotic body horror version of *The Blob*. **158 pages $11**

BB-150 **"Tentacle Death Trip" Jordan Krall** — It's *Death Race 2000* meets H. P. Lovecraft in bizarro author Jordan Krall's best and most suspenseful work to date. **224 pages $12**

BB-151 **"The Obese" Nick Antosca** — Like Alfred Hitchcock's *The Birds*... but with obese people. **108 pages $10**

BB-152 **"All-Monster Action!" Cody Goodfellow** — The world gave him a blank check and a demand: Create giant monsters to fight our wars. But Dr. Otaku was not satisfied with mere chaos and mass destruction.... **216 pages $12**

BB-153 **"Ugly Heaven" Carlton Mellick III** — Heaven is no longer a paradise. It was once a blissful utopia full of wonders far beyond human comprehension. But the afterlife is now in ruins. It has become an ugly, lonely wasteland populated by strange monstrous beasts, masturbating angels, and sad man-like beings wallowing in the remains of the once-great Kingdom of God. **106 pages $8**

BB-154 **"Space Walrus" Kevin L. Donihe** — Walter is supposed to go where no walrus has ever gone before, but all this astronaut walrus really wants is to take it easy on the intense training, escape the chimpanzee bullies, and win the love of his human trainer Dr. Stephanie. **160 pages $11**